JUBILEE

JESSICA LEE WRIGHT

For My Grandparents,

Herman and Helen Bick

and

Samuel and Sadie Sacharow

And for my parents,

Sidney and Lillian Beck

```
"
```

Table of Contents

Extract: Leviticus 25

8And thou shalt number seven sabbaths of years unto thee, seven times seven years; and there shall be unto thee the days of seven sabbaths of years, every forty and nine years.

9Then shalt thou make proclamation with the blast of the horn on the tenth day of the seventh month; in the day of atonement shall ye make proclamation with the horn throughout all your land.

10And ye shall hallow the fiftieth year, and proclaim liberty throughput the land unto all the inhabitants thereof; it shall be a jubilee unto you; and ye shall return every man unto his possession, and ye shall return every man unto his family.

PROLOGUE

It was a cold winter in America. It wasn't just the weather, which was bleak and frigid for much of the country in the second week of January, in the year 2033. The mood of the people was steadily declining as hopes for the future dimmed. So many were out of work and it was becoming harder for the government to provide assistance to the tens of millions who had nothing. In every town and city in the nation people were camped out in parks and on sidewalks, using cardboard boxes for shelter. Having been evicted for nonpayment of rent and taxes, long time residents refused to leave their places of birth. The buildings they had called home lay empty and in disrepair because local government coffers were depleted. In many cities around the country, demonstrations by people demanding the government do something to address the poverty, crime and poor living conditions in the sprawling slums, occurred weekly, often ending in rioting and looting. Morale was low in the ranks of the police who often had to be backed up by National Guard troops to control the angry mobs.

Heavy borrowing from China, the world's biggest economy, had been in progress for decades. Trillions lent became tens of trillions as the interest on the debt grew. Plans for repayment were never given much consideration. The United States had begun to be seen as a debtor nation around the world. This was a status inherently devastating to the ethos of a people who revered independence. The long recession of the early 2000's had never really ended for the vast majority of Americans despite rosy data put out by most in the media. People eventually stopped listening. They knew they were being told half-truths at best. Most just wanted their leaders to be frank with them. That was the only way anyone could hope to devise a way out of the morass that had been created.

It was in this atmosphere of distrust and frustration that James Gengia, Republican congressman from New York, had been elected president of the United States of America in 2032. One year later, as he sat at his desk in the Oval Office, he addressed the nation:

PART ONE

Chapter One
"MY FELLOW AMERICANS

I come before you today to give important news, news that will surprise everyone, and which will require some time to grasp.

I will start by recounting a little ancient history which may help to put today's events into historical context and provide a rationale for what has unfolded. Several thousand years ago, in biblical times, our forebears were subject to religious law whereby a system of debt-forgiveness was legitimized. This law was simple and deliberate. It was organized by time and place and it affected all people who participated in economic society.

Every forty-nine years, roughly a lifetime at that time, all debt was forgiven. Debts, at the time, varied. One could owe a camel or a horse to someone who had provided chickens. Someone else might have owed milk to a fruit farmer. Currency, though not made of paper, might have been owed to those who performed physical labor.

The year in which all debts were forgiven was called 'The Year of Jubilee'. I am happy to tell you today that in a stunningly generous act, and in the interest of world peace and prosperity, the government of The People's Republic of China has enacted a 'Day of Jubilee'. By doing so, they have effectively cancelled all United States government debt owed to them. As you know, the amount of debt previously owed was upwards of one hundred trillion dollars. It is now zero.

As you take in this news, you will undoubtedly have many

questions. I will do my best, in the coming days, to answer them. I, too, am still digesting all the implications of this unprecedented act of enormous goodwill."

As president Gengia spoke to the nation, he could feel the warmth and spirit of those gathered around him; the friends and family who had joined him along the way as his journey to this day progressed. His thoughts turned to his counterpart in Beijing as he supposed that a similar speech would be made by his closest and most trusted friend, Chan Khan, the president of China.

Both men, young, and new to the world as leaders, were completely focused on the days ahead and the momentous consequences of their actions.

The life histories that led to the events of that day belie the notion of predictable destiny. For who can delve into the humble beginnings of great men without marveling at known outcomes. Each person starts life as a small, dependent, vulnerable creature. Any little danger can end in annihilation. It is, therefore, a miracle that we humans live to become anything at all, let alone heroes among men.

Chapter Two

In the spring of 1988, Sonia Gengia, a seventeen year old living in a tiny row house with her mother Marie in a small town in upstate New York, became pregnant by Mark, her classmate and her only confidant. They had dated on and off throughout their last year of high school and Sonia had developed real feelings for him. Though he had allowed the relationship to become physical, Mark was really only interested in Sonia as a close friend. He was eager to have someone to commiserate with about the boredom of their provincial lives, but he was far from wanting a serious romantic involvement. By the end of the school year, he broke off from her permanently. He did not know, at the time, that he was to become a father.

Sonia had never met her own father; he'd died when she was an infant. The stories her mother told her about him left her with romantic notions of their beautiful marriage. This narrative seemed to fit with the fact that Marie - who was only in her twenties when she became a widow - never pursued another relationship. She told anyone who asked that she doubted she would ever recover from the loss of her first love. Sonia, in turn, grew up revering her father's memory and feeling great sympathy for her mother's bad fortune.

When she began elementary school, Sonia was an eager student. It was her only outlet for learning and exploration outside the home and she treasured it. She carefully prepared each morning for the day ahead, making sure her clothes were clean and pressed, her lunch was packed and her arrival was on time. Bright and willing in class, her schoolmates dubbed her "teacher's pet". Her mother, however, was much less keen on Sonia's educational career. She discouraged her little girl at every turn, reminding her each day that she would someday become a wife and mother and that these were the roles for which she needed to prepare.

Marie did not believe that girls should be educated beyond the basics. She firmly held that a woman's place was in the home, preferably deferring all major decisions to a man. This was how she had been raised. Though she knew her own lack of schooling had left her unprepared to cope when she lost her husband, she rigidly clung to her old, familiar beliefs. Sonia took in her mother's words but she couldn't understand how enjoying her friends at school, pleasing her teachers and learning new skills would interfere with her future as a housewife and mother. She pressed on with her daily routine, hiding her enthusiasm from Marie.

As Sonia entered high school she was weighed down with household responsibilities. Her mother saw to it that she had little time to read and do homework. She began to hide her schoolwork by doing it surreptitiously in her room at night. She could barely stay awake in the dim light as she crammed for tests and wrote papers while hiding books under the covers. As the assignments became more taxing and time consuming, the young student often fell behind and her grades declined. She felt she couldn't compete with her peers who, with the help of supportive families, devoted their afternoons and evenings to their studies.

Slowly Sonia became increasingly disheartened as her teachers, who once viewed her as the most promising student, seemed to lose interest in her. Believing that she would not have the necessary resources to succeed as school progressed, she began to lose hope in what seemed like a lost cause until she finally gave in to her mother and put any thought of educational success out of her mind. Feeling personally defeated and overpowered by her mother, Sonia allowed her attention to be diverted to the amusing activities of her fellow students. She was at an age when boys and dating were becoming intriguing topics among her female classmates. Though not part of the popular crowd, she learned how to fit in by feigning an agreeable, outgoing front. Soon she found herself mingling with the more socially active girls in her grade, the ones interested in finding a boyfriend. It was during this phase that she noticed the adorable freckled boy sitting beside her in homeroom.

Mark was funny, always ready with a quip. Each day, as Sonia made her way to her desk, he narrowed his eyes and commented in a mockingly serious voice, "The demure Miss Sonia has arrived." Her inclination was to ignore his routine, but as time went on, she gave him the occasional rolled eye and, eventually, a smile. With this little bit of encouragement he began talking to the quiet, petite brunette at the adjacent desk. They soon became friends. As she got to know Mark, Sonia realized that he used his wit to hide feelings of constriction and suppression. His daily existence was dictated by his religious family's rules and rituals. His own desires and fantasies were stifled to accommodate others. Underneath the lighthearted banter was a frustrated, lonely boy who sought someone his age, someone outside his family. They began opening up to each other in ways neither had before. Mark was mystified by Sonia's recounting of her mother's attitude toward learning. It was the exact opposite of the pressure he faced at home to succeed. His father's command to "study harder" played in his mind as a recorded message he could not erase. The beleaguered teens comforted each other and found refuge from their parents' scrutiny.

It wasn't long before the pair decided to meet after school on the pretext of continuing an ongoing discussion. Mark found Sonia so easy to be with. She was sweet and unaffected, unlike the other girls he knew. She made few demands, allowing him to steer their relationship wherever he saw fit. He found himself wanting to sit close to his new friend and he was encouraged when she didn't back away. The two spent as much time as they could together, stealing an hour here and there after school away from their parents' close watch. They often met at the local diner, sharing milkshakes and sundaes and close personal secrets. Sonia revealed that she had never been intimate with a boy. She asked Mark to tell her what he knew about male/female relations. He was happy to tutor her on the subject and this soon became their favorite topic of conversation. Their increasing physical attraction clouded their better judgment and one day the pair found themselves alone in Mark's room while his parents were out. They undressed and awkwardly fell onto his bed. Once the lovemaking had begun, there was no going back. They found a way to meet almost every week. As the months went by and the initial sexual fervor cooled, Mark began to realize that their behavior was extremely risky. He worried that they were both uncertain about methods of birth control and that their trysts could result in an unwanted pregnancy. Though he hated the idea of losing the only person he had ever intimately known, he felt that the best way to end it was to completely break off from Sonia. Her reaction was total bewilderment. She couldn't understand why he wasn't missing her and all the closeness they shared. She felt rejected and discarded. She wondered if he had ever felt the joy she had felt while they were alone together. She assumed his love had just been an illusion, something she created in her mind to alleviate her boring existence.

A few months after their breakup came the realization that their relationship would have consequences beyond her feelings of hurt and sorrow.

Sonia was too ashamed and afraid to tell her single, poverty stricken mother that she was pregnant. She had no money of her own and she was so confused and upset about the predicament that she denied to herself that it was true. As the months went by, Sonia watched, with increasing dread, her body change. She had gone from a lanky, awkward teen to a fully filled out woman and then to an obvious mother-to-be. Though she was still slender, her hips expanded and her breasts grew to the point that her clothes no longer fit. Not able to buy new things, Sonia had no choice but to wear baggy sweat shirts over her protruding belly. She began staying home from school and was often too embarrassed to leave the house. Every day Sonia woke in fear that her pregnancy was gradually becoming more and more apparent. So many times she steeled herself and approached her mother with the news of her condition only to back down at the last minute and retreat in silence. Marie was always too preoccupied with her own worries to notice the changes in her daughter. She was glad to have the extra help with chores when her daughter missed school. Sonia was aware that there was a small window of time in which to decide if she wanted to terminate her pregnancy. She knew she was rapidly reaching the point of no return. The thought of ending the life inside her body was so abhorrent to this gentle, sensitive girl that she eventually resigned herself to her fate.

Though reluctant and fearful, Sonia was to become a mother. She never told Mark about the baby because she felt he couldn't help her, being a poor teenager himself. When Marie finally sensed what was happening, she hid her face in shame. She assumed it was the result of her bad parenting along with her usual bad luck. She made Sonia promise to keep the pregnancy a secret for as long as she could. This meant that the expectant teenager had to avoid being seen in public. Daylight hours were spent doing indoor chores. If she needed to go out, Sonia waited until nightfall and wore a loose raincoat to hide her expanding waistline. She cut herself off from friends once the school year ended. Some of her former classmates grew suspicious and rumors abounded. Mother and daughter were alone and scared. How would they cope with a new mouth to feed? What would become of the child? They cried together as they looked toward an even more uncertain future. And yet there was something hopeful about a new life that even they couldn't deny. They started making meager plans for the baby's arrival.

Chapter Three

Half a world away, Sulee Khan was living in a secret cellar on a small farm in southwestern China. Her father, Anlee, along with her husband, Aro, had dug out the hiding place with their crude tools. They worked every night to create a hiding place for Sulee. After three weeks of digging and two weeks of plastering, they completed the six by eight foot room and ushered the pregnant young woman down a ladder and into her new home.

With the help of her uncle, Luang, who was the local doctor, Sulee's family faked her death and began the long ordeal of helping her conceive her illegal second child, Chan. China's one-child policy had been in effect for ten years. There were severe punishments in many provinces, including their own, for those who violated the law. Often expectant mothers were forced to undergo abortions. For this reason, the terrified couple chose to stage an elaborate ruse to safeguard mother and child. Sulee's elder child, one year-old Hanlee, would now be raised by Aro. She would be told that Mother died young, but had loved her dearly.

Beyond the new baby's birth, Sulee and her family had no plan. They knew they were risking their lives by breaking the law, but they believed in their hearts that this baby must be allowed to live. There was complete agreement and therefore they resolutely went forward with unwavering commitment to the task.

Chapter Four

Back in New York, Sonia prepared to have her baby. She and her mother assumed it would be a girl for no other reason than that they knew nothing about the raising of a boy. They were so sure, they never chose any male names. They agreed to name the baby Rosalie, after Marie's mother. The few clothing items they bought in anticipation of the birth were pink and frilly. Together they scoured garage sales and secondhand shops for the crib and accessories their new baby girl would need. Sonia quickly understood that her mother was enjoying all the preparations they were making for the baby. She realized that Marie saw this as a woman's natural role, as she had always said. Sonia was so happy to finally have the chance to fulfill her mother's ideals. The two women began to share a relaxed and pleasing closeness. They did their best to create a suitable nursery for little Rosalie. She would be the third generation of Gengia women and though they both wanted to give her a warm and comfortable beginning, they doubted her life would be any better than theirs had been.

The birth day came and Sonia took her time before heading to the hospital. She was so fearful of the ordeal that lay ahead of her. Finally, she told her mother, "It's time." They made a mad dash in a cab to the emergency room. The nurses gave Sonia a quick examination and rushed her to the delivery room. The baby was coming. When the doctor arrived, he assessed the situation and immediately administered ether; it was too late for the usual procedure of numbing below the waist. Sonia woke one half hour later and saw the baby being bundled into a blanket in the nurse's arms. The nurse turned to her and said, "Congratulations! It's a beautiful baby boy!" Sonia looked at her, then at the baby and then around the room searching for her mother. She couldn't believe what the nurse had said. She needed confirmation, but Marie was nowhere in sight. The nurse handed her the warm bundle and unwrapped him to show Sonia that he was indeed beautiful and indeed a boy. Tears began to fall and they would not stop. It seemed to Sonia that a great unknown wish had been granted. She was overwhelmed with new emotions that she could not name. She looked at the baby and realized that she had to pull herself together as not to scare him. She smiled at him as she kissed his tiny face.

When Marie entered the room, Sonia, whose eyes were riveted on her new son, simply said, "I have a boy."

"A boy? What will we name him?"

Sonia didn't hesitate. "James, after my father."

"That's a wonderful idea! Thank you Sonia. May I look? Oh, he's just perfect." In her sweetest softest voice she cooed, "Welcome little James. I'm your grandma."

The two women raised the boy with great financial and emotional difficulty. The joy they had experienced at James' birth could not be sustained in the face of the daily drudgery of their lives. There was never enough money for necessities, so they went without, often subsisting on meager meals and living in barely heated rooms. As a result, James was always sick with minor childhood illnesses. Sonia had no life outside her small family.

She loved little James - whom she imagined took after her father's looks - but she also resented him at times and felt her life had been interrupted. And so she was an ambivalent mother, starting and ending her days gazing into her son's mysteriously mesmerizing eyes, while dreading all she had to do to meet his never-ending needs.

As a young teenager, Sonia had fantasized about becoming a television personality, maybe a talk show host. She and Mark had long, dreamy conversations about their possible careers.

They both found the media industry exciting and sexy, the exact opposite of their everyday lives.

For Sonia, that was now out of the question. She buried her dreams and began living day to day. She couldn't even go on after graduation from high school because her depressed, overworked mother was too overwhelmed to babysit for little James. The future for Sonia and Marie seemed to hold little hope. Whether out of fear or timidity, they would not allow themselves to imagine a new path. The looming world did not beckon this mother and daughter. They hid from its dangers by creating a smaller and smaller existence.

Chapter Five

Months before Chan's birth, Sulee slowly began to adjust to her underground cell. She remembered the fateful day when, after realizing she was pregnant, she sat for hours wondering how she would tell Aro. What would she say? She now had plenty of time, nothing but time, to recount her life, her marriage, and to worry about the future. She thought back to the day she had met Aro. He was a newcomer to the small, agricultural town in southwest China where she had always lived. He arrived with his mother; his father had died the previous year. He had been promised a job at the furniture factory just outside of town.

Aro Khan was tall and strong, unlike the local men. Sulee was standing outside the food commune when she first saw him. He stood out because of his height and heft, but there was something else. Aro did not look Chinese. He had rounder eyes than most, and his skin was swarthier. His nose was wide and he had a broad chin. Sulee thought he was extremely attractive, and for the first time in her young life, she was infatuated with a man.

Now, several years later, she sat scared and cold in a dank cell. Somewhere in her distant memory she recalled feeling as alone as she did now. When she was only two years old, her mother, Ling Chi, died of dengue fever. At the time, Uncle Luang was making the transition from herbalist to doctor. In his small, poor, rural community, he was the only one to turn to for help with illness. He had worked feverishly to save his sister, but to no avail. Luang promised Ling Chi, on her deathbed, that he would help Anlee with the raising of the child, and he was as good as his word. Sulee came to see him as her "second father". Because of his high regard in the village, she tended to identify with him more than her quiet, retiring father, the lonely, reticent man who had given her life. It was no surprise, therefore, that she put her faith in her uncle to save her and her unborn child from severe, inhumane punishment.

Chapter Six

Dr. Luang had always been a practical person. He was frugal and had a knack for making do and stretching his resources to their fullest use. Having grown up on a farm, he loved to grow his own food and mend his worn clothing. He lived a simple life, forgoing life's extravagances as he thought they got in the way of the important goals he was always setting for himself. He had a grand scheme for his future as an herbalist and a doctor. Each day he made a list of tasks to be done in order of importance. Luang rarely failed to complete his self imposed assignments. His parents marveled at his tenacity. Though they had named him Chan at birth, it wasn't long before his adoring mother nicknamed him ChiChi. Not long after that, he rejected the pet name, preferring at school and elsewhere to just be called "Luang". He considered having two names superfluous. One name would suffice for him.

As a boy, Luang had a serious demeanor. He didn't lack joy - he had a warm smile and an engaging soft voice. His keen focus and passion for learning, however, left little room for frivolity.

When his father took him to the herb gardens and taught him about the ancient remedies which his own father had passed on to him, Luang absorbed the knowledge with a religious fervor. He immediately grasped the concept of curing as a noble pursuit. Once on this path, he was not easily diverted. As a result, he was a solitary child. He loved his roly-poly baby sister, but play did not come easily to him and he was relieved that his mother had quit doting on him and had turned her attention to little Ling Chi.

Luang knew everyone in his village and he conveyed an interest in their lives, asking after his neighbors' family members and expressing concern about their general well-being. Other than casual conversations, however, he had an aura of detachment from the social community.

Classmates at school sensed that he was preoccupied by his studies. They left him, respectfully, to his work. Embedded in his ancient Chinese culture, which has prevailed regardless of regime, is the notion that one's livelihood is a central part of one's identity. Being a worthwhile person requires being serious about work. Hence, Luang, though remote and reserved, was respected by everyone who knew him.

Of course, some were frustrated by his unavailability. Girls his age tried desperately to get his attention. They saw him as a challenge, and it didn't hurt that he was handsomer and taller than most. He often got into trouble by kindly rejecting them, one by one. He admired the opposite sex, but he knew that the flower of his heart would not be picked until he had his major achievements behind him. There was one in the group, Myong, who was more persistent than the others. She followed Luang at school, dropping books, coughing, calling out to friends, all to get his attention. She often walked by his home, hoping he would be out in his herb garden.

Then she would amble over to him, ask questions, and generally act like a pest. Sometimes she hid behind a tree for hours and watched him work. Luang tried to ignore her but Myong was relentless.

One day, as he walked toward town, he heard footsteps behind him. He looked back and saw Myong gaining on him. She was a large boned, hefty girl with an unpleasant, determined demeanor. Her big feet tromped heavily on the well worn ground beneath them, arousing apprehension in any living thing in her path. At first, Luang began to walk faster. He thought she would get the hint and turn around. His heart was beating hard as he heard her coming closer. He could hear her breathing. She called out, "Luang!"

He turned, looked at her, and stopped.

"What is it Myong?"

"Why are you running away from me? I want to talk to you."

"What about?"

"I invited you to my birthday celebration and you never responded. I want to know if you're coming."

"No, I can't come. I'm busy that day."

"What day?"

"The day of your birthday."

"What day is it on?"

"I'm not sure."

"Just as I thought. How could you know you're busy if you don't know the date?"

"Myong, I'm not interested in parties."

"No, you're not interested in me! Do you think I'm ugly or something? Why do you always run away from me? I really like you. We could be a couple. I know you would like me if you'd give me a chance."

"I like you but I'm not interested in being a couple."

"Why not? Do you like boys? If you don't come to my party, I'll have to decide that you like boys. Everyone will know. Don't expect me to keep it a secret!"

"Is this your way of making me like you?"

"Now you're being mean. Do you want to be known as a mean boy who favors other boys?

One word from me and the whole town will know."

"All this so I'll come to your party?"

"I like to get my way."

"You'll ruin my name just to get your way?"

"Of course you know I'm kidding. Say you'll come and we'll forget everything else."

"How could I refuse, Myong?"

Walking quickly from her, he feared to look back. This girl was trouble and there was no way to avoid her in their small village. Maybe he should let everyone think he liked boys. The trouble was, there were a few girls Luang had his eye on for the future. The distant future. One of them was Myong's younger sister, Mae Ling. She was the opposite of Myong in almost every way. She was a beautiful, petite creature whose sweet nature was no match for her overbearing sister. She shrunk in Myong's presence. Luang loved her delicate features and soft voice. Her timidity made him feel strong and masculine. He had the urge to protect her, especially from her big, loud sister. If he ever decided the time was right to pursue Mae Ling, he knew it would put her in the path of the wrath of Myong. For now, he would admire her from a distance. In the meantime, he would have to figure out how to cope with Myong's constant harassment and stalking. This quiet, reserved teenager couldn't understand her obsession.

Having avoided socializing with his peers, Luang was ill equipped to deal with this love struck tormentor. Now he was beginning to get a sense of the ire of a scorned suitor. Devising a way to fend off someone who threatened to upset his world was a new experience. What he didn't know was that this would not be the last time Myong would threaten his plans.

Luang went on with his life, tending to his herbs with care, constantly trying to improve them by studying horticulture. He was also a student of language. He knew that most medical journals were written in languages other than Chinese. As a rule, the latest scientific breakthroughs were not readily available to the people of rural China. Luang did his best to obtain journals and pamphlets dealing with herbal medicine, but the information he was able to get was always years old. He would travel for days in a wooden cart, powered by his donkey, to the nearest large city and visit doctors who knew him and lent him their newest material.

Together they would spend hours teaching themselves to speak and read English and French.

As Luang matured and reached adulthood, he began applying his knowledge to the practice his ancestors had begun. He saw his fellow countrymen dying in droves from one disease or another, but the one that took the most lives was the dreaded dengue fever. This deadly plague had been a terrible scourge throughout the East for centuries. Now it was being identified more readily by doctors around the world. It eluded all attempts at a cure. Luang worked in his makeshift laboratory in a group of crude huts which had been built by his father. Each hut had four beds and, as the years went by, his small clinic was usually filled to capacity, mostly with dengue fever victims. Luang worked tirelessly ministering to his patients but no one was saved in his rudimentary hospital. Whole families were wiped out every year. When his own sister, Ling Chi, died in his arms at the age of twenty three, Luang despaired of ever finding a way to heal anyone. He had tried every herbal combination he knew to cure her. He could not. She died leaving behind her two year old daughter, Sulee. Along with his promise to help look after the child, he vowed to himself to redouble his efforts in battling the disease.

Chapter Seven

Sulee was a beautiful little girl with big dark eyes and long, shiny black hair. Her childhood was happy, despite the absence of a mother, because she was loved and cared for by her father and uncle. She felt somewhat privileged in her community as she was related to the esteemed Dr. Luang. She grew up loving her two "fathers". Anlee was a kindhearted survivor whose acute senses taught him to be obscure in his unpredictable environment. Because he found it tedious and futile to try to comply with the ever changing governmental rules and regulations, he avoided any interaction he believed might lead to trouble with the powers that be. Other than raising his daughter, he lived a solitary life, spending his days reading and weaving baskets which he sold along the road in his neighborhood. The other person in Sulee's life was also kind, but that was where the similarity ended. Her uncle lived his life in a systematic, determined way. He saw the dangers around him and his family as puzzles waiting to be solved. He was usually able to outwit anyone or anything threatening to impede his plans.

Luang remained a single man, devoting himself to work and forgoing the opportunity to marry Mae Ling when she came of age. Though she returned his smiles, she realized that the two of them had better not try to go up against Myong. She had no trouble finding a mate and married a local man, much to the disappointment of Luang. He knew he had relinquished his chance, but, considering the obstacles they might face, he assumed it was for the best.

As a teenager, Sulee was protected from suitors by the two men carefully watching over her.

No one was allowed close to her, and certainly, no one was allowed to be alone with her. When she met and fell in love with Aro Khan, there was panic in the household. Her father followed the couple relentlessly. Uncle Luang investigated Aro's family. What he discovered was that Aro was only half Chinese. His father was Mongolian and was rumored to be a direct descendant of the great Mongol warrior, Genghis Khan. This was difficult for Luang to believe as Aro was a sweet and gentle man with no obvious signs of aggression or egoism. He began stopping by their home every night after work and was usually asked to join them for their evening meal. There was always something that needed fixing in the dilapidated house and Aro cheerfully obliged. Anlee began saving up his household chores so the helpful young suitor could give him a hand.

After many months of observing the happy couple hand in hand as they quietly walked and talked together around the village, the "fathers" exchanged their views on the situation. As they sipped their evening tea alone in the small garden adjacent to the hospital, Anlee opened the dialogue by musing about Sulee's future.

"You and Sulee have been working together for some time now. What do you think of her ability as a nurse, brother?"

"I continue to be impressed by her dedication and her desire to absorb knowledge. She now speaks three languages and studies all the material we receive from around the world. You have raised a caring and capable girl, Anlee. You can be proud."

"We both deserve the credit! Do not sell yourself short. I doubt I could have raised her alone. I am eternally grateful to you and so is she. Have you discussed further studies or training with her? Is it enough to keep things as they are or do you think we should encourage her to seek more formal education?"

Luang considered this question for a moment. He let out a chuckle as he noted, "I'm not sure Sulee would agree to leave the village right now. The nearest university is hours away and we both know she would vehemently protest leaving her close friend Aro for any reason."

Anlee feigned shock. "We can't allow her to stymie her education for a silly romantic crush!

She's too young to pick a mate for life."

Luang gave his brother-in-law an incredulous look. "Are you forgetting that you and my sister were betrothed when you were two years younger than Sulee?"

"We were much more mature." Anlee protested.

"Or at least you thought you were." Luang shot back. "We can't ignore the fact that Sulee has made herself exclusively available to Aro and that he spends as much time around her as he can. If this is not true love, it's a very good imitation!"

"I admit they look happy together." Mused Anlee. "I am fond of Aro. I see that he is an able and helpful sort. I, myself, have gotten used to having an extra pair of strong hands around the house. We could do worse with another unknown man, I suppose. But if he wants to continue to take up all my daughter's time he must declare his intentions soon. I'm her father. I'm responsible for her future. I want to know which way she is headed in life."

"Then perhaps you should speak to him and let him know how you feel," suggested Luang.

"I intend to do just that!" Anlee retorted loudly.

Not surprisingly, Anlee's concerns were also weighing on the mind of Aro. Days before the fathers talked, he broached the subject of their future with the woman he loved. During a walk that took them far enough away from the village to ensure privacy, Aro turned to Sulee and said in a serious tone, "If I had my way we would continue walking together for the rest of our lives."

"That would be lovely." She responded modestly.

"Do you mean that, my darling?" He asked, turning abruptly toward her. "Because, if you do, I'll take it as an acceptance of my proposal of marriage."

"Don't you intend to get down on one knee, take my hand and beg me to be your wife?"

At that, Aro dropped to the ground and performed the ritual. "My beautiful love and my best friend, Sulee, will you marry me?"

The delighted girl stifled a giggle and accepted with an exuberant "Yes, yes. I will marry you."

"You just gave me the most happiness I've ever felt! To know that we will always be together is to see a future that is my dream come true. I am the luckiest man alive!" he exclaimed as he lifted his bride-to-be in the air and twirled her around. "Now we must quickly make our way back home so I can ask your father for his consent. I don't want to waste a minute in case you change your mind!"

As they started to run toward her house, Sulee assured him, "That will not happen, Aro my love.

I have also dreamt of this day."

The two were out of breath when they finally reached the hut. Aro turned toward his beloved and asked, "Will you wait here while I go inside? I don't want you to be there in case he says no."

"I would much rather we faced father together, my darling. Don't worry! He and uncle speak highly of you. They have warmed to you over these past months. He will consent. You will see."

They walked through the door together and saw Anlee staring at the fire, lost in thought. When he looked up and saw the beaming couple, he smiled warmly and they instantly knew he would give them his blessing. Aro spoke up. "I have come to ask you, respectfully, for your daughter's hand in marriage. I love her very much and with your consent, I will honor and care for her for the remainder of my days."

Anlee looked at his daughter and asked, "Is this your wish as well?"

"Oh yes, father!" she replied clasping her hands together.

"Then I must open a very old bottle of spirits which I have been saving for a happy occasion like this. But first let me shake your hand, Aro, and welcome you to our family. You have my blessing."

Just as the glasses were raised for a toast, in walked Luang. Sulee's happiness was now complete. She was surrounded by all the men who loved her. Anlee put his arm around his daughter as he faced her betrothed.

"May my new son Aro and my cherished Sulee have a long and fruitful life."

Not long after, the young couple married and began living a quiet, happy life. Working alongside her uncle in the hospital, Sulee honed her nursing skills and continued to improve her proficiency with the languages he spoke and read. Aro became a furniture craftsman in the local factory. Within two years, their daughter, Hanlee, was born. The new parents knew comfort and calm until one day, in their third year of marriage, when Sulee began to feel lightheaded and weak after waking each morning. She told no one and tried to brush it off. She forced herself to eat and rest, but the lethargy and fatigue worsened. In a month she knew that what she feared was true, she was pregnant.

Watching in quiet amazement, Aro remembered the day Sulee told him she was expecting again. His beautiful wife was waiting for him after his long day of work. There were tears in her eyes and an almost haunted look on her face. As she told him the news, she let her emotions spill out and she collapsed, crying in his arms. Aro cried too. They held each other tightly but they could not see beyond their tears.

After his initial reaction of surprise when he learned Sulee was expecting again, Aro's emotions immediately turned to fear and then terror when he realized what would befall his wife and the new life inside her. Though a new baby boy would be tolerated by the powers that be, another girl would be illegal. If it was discovered that she was pregnant again, she might be forced to abort the baby she was carrying. Aro and Sulee instinctively turned to Uncle Luang because they knew he was the one person who could be trusted to find the best way out of what could become a calamity. Their little family had been so content since their marriage and the birth of Hanlee. Aro knew those carefree days were never to be had again and he felt powerless to protect and defend the destiny of his wife and children.

The young couple was now facing an unknown, frightening future. They looked at their happy, chubby little girl and, without saying a word, they both knew they would be risking her safety and security if they decided to keep their new child alive. An agonizing choice had to be made. They felt trapped and paralyzed and unable to think clearly. Sulee and Aro realized they needed the help of those they loved and trusted. But was it fair to involve the whole family in their impossible situation. What right did they have to put them in danger? Then again, how could they find a solution without them?

Together they walked slowly down the dirt path to the long, low tin structures which made up the medical clinic. Luang was inside, working alone. When he saw their faces, he knew trouble had come.

"Good evening children. My my, you do look serious. How can I help?"

"We have a serious problem, indeed, Uncle," Aro said quietly. "Sulee is expecting."

Luang felt like he had been punched in the stomach. It was hard for him to get air. He looked at Sulee. He could see she had been crying.

"Come and sit by me Sulee. Tell me what you're thinking."

"I've wracked my brain since the moment I realized I was with child. Not knowing which way to turn, I went to mother's grave to seek her silent guidance. I sat with her for hours but heard nothing. My mind drifted far up into the heavens and, when I looked back at mother's tombstone, instead of her name and the dates of her birth and death, it read,

'Baby of mine,

You will always be with me,

No matter where I go.

Hanlee came and grew,

Then she flew,

Always hovering nearby,

Living and loving to my heart's delight.

But you are unsettled,

Neither here nor there.

I reach for you,

But to no avail.

My heart is your slave.'

When I came out of my reverie, I knew that mother had spoken. I knew my baby must be born."

Uncle Luang listened to the couple with increasing alarm. The situation was even more perilous than they realized. He had seen the fierce tactics employed by the government when it came to illegal births. He spoke to the couple calmly though his heart was full of dread.

"You are both young and brave and that is good because you will need every ounce of strength and courage now that you have decided to keep this child alive. I will need some time to think.

Right now I'm not prepared to give you any advice other than to tell no one else. Try to conduct yourselves as if all is normal and usual. Come and see me in two days and we will devise a plan of action. I will be by your side always. No more crying. Save your strength for what lies ahead."

He hugged Sulee and then Aro and sent them on their way. He knew he could waste no time.

He quickly ran out of the hospital and went looking for Anlee. He found Sulee's father asleep in his hut. Luang woke him, filled him in, and the two stayed up all night planning. What they came up with would require total secrecy and cooperation from Aro and Sulee. It would be extremely hard on both. The next morning they went together to propose their scheme to the couple. There was no hesitation. The family agreed to move ahead immediately.

Chapter Eight

During her second month of pregnancy, Sulee experienced extreme bouts of morning sickness. Her inability to eat, constant nausea and fatigue made her gaunt and sickly looking. Uncle Luang noticed this and immediately saw it as an opportunity to put his plan in effect. He spread rumors around the village that Sulee had contracted dengue fever. He put her in bed, where she became even more pallid and wan. Some of the more inquisitive old women who lived nearby risked their health to see for themselves, just as Luang hoped they would. Of course Myong was among the busy bodies. For reasons she herself couldn't grasp, she was skeptical about Sulee's sudden illness. She wanted visible proof. She shamelessly strode into the sick room with her friends in tow. She peered into the face of the ailing young woman and was about to poke her belly when Luang stepped in to stop her.

"I wouldn't touch her if I were you. She's highly contagious. You'll have only yourself to blame if you contract the disease, Myong!"

Sulee held up her part of the act, coughing and moaning and seeming to writhe in pain. The visiting gawkers were amazed to see this once beautiful, plump, young woman looking so pale and disease stricken. They were not surprised, therefore, when one week into her "illness", she was pronounced dead. After the feigned funeral and burial, Sulee began her underground vigil.

Constructing a bunker for Sulee was a project fraught with danger. The three men who took on the job had to decide on a location which could be accessed easily so that food, water and other essentials could be delivered when necessary. They opted to locate the hiding place on the grounds of the hospital. Because Luang lived there and had complete control over the clinic, they knew he would be free to see his niece as needed. It was also imperative that he be close by to deliver her baby when the time came.

There was a root cellar under one of the huts at the far end of the hospital. It was decided that they would enlarge this space and create a hidden door to the new hideaway. This plan allowed them to use the existing stairway and to store supplies in the front room. To avoid the appearance of suspicious activity in the area, all agreed that only Luang would visit Sulee.

Silently working side by side at night, the men thought about the possible consequences of their actions. They knew that if they were found out, they would most likely be punished with prison or worse. For Luang, this was the first time in his life that he had ventured into the realm of illegal activity. He considered himself a righteous man, a pillar of society who, above all, strove to do no harm. He could not allow others, however, to harm Sulee and her child. He had vowed to protect her and he felt his duty to her and to his sister came before any other consideration. Anlee had few qualms when it came to breaking the law. He viewed many of the government's rules as arbitrary and inconsistent. This was not the first time he had skirted the authorities and he knew it would not be the last. His only concern, at present, was the safety and security of his daughter and future grandchild. The last of the three, Aro, was tormented and torn. With every thrust of his shovel, he felt his beautiful wife slipping further from him. The labor made his arms ache but it was the pain in his heart that caused tears to fall down his cheeks.

There was no glory for any of them in the completion of their work. Aro arrived home in the wee hours and saw Sulee sleeping peacefully alongside their daughter. He stood in the room staring at the lovely scene for several minutes. He was trying to create a memory which he knew he would need to sustain him.

The next day, Sulee gathered the clothes and personal items she considered most essential. She solemnly kissed Aro and Hanlee goodbye and walked alone to the hospital, uncertain if she would ever see them again.

Chapter Nine

With Sulee gone, Luang was working alone in his clinic. He missed having a helper but with his worry about the plot he was orchestrating, he was in no mood to train and supervise a new nurse. Eventually, however, he agreed to hire a young widow from the village named Xin. She was the daughter of his not forgotten love, Mae Ling, and the niece of Myong. Xin had an infant son, Mi. She had lost her husband in one of the many work-related accidents that occurred in the logging industry. Xin worked diligently alongside the doctor, freeing him up to think creatively and in new directions. He came to realize that many of the deaths he was seeing around him were due to variants of dengue fever. He began studying the early symptoms by assuming that anyone feeling ill might be coming down with the fever. He then sorted the sick into two groupings. One group contained those who went on to develop the disease. The other group included people who had another, unrelated Illness. After discovering which initial ailments usually resulted in a dengue fever diagnosis, he immediately began dosing those he considered most at risk with a medicinal "cocktail" made up of precise variations of herbal combinations. After continual trial and error, the disease began to yield to his newest concoction.

Only a few months after Sulee's departure from her above ground family, life for Aro took a turn for the worse. When Luang devised the plan to hide Sulee after her "death", he failed to anticipate the consequences of Aro's new single status. There were several village widows with children who were vulnerable and needed protection and care. It wasn't long before Aro was urged to do his part and pick from the group of local unmarrieds. Of course, Myong pushed for him to wed her niece, Xin. Always the schemer, she let it be known that Xin was the obvious favorite due to her position as Dr. Luang's nurse. "After all," she told everyone, "Aro already knows her and her son, Mi. They're practically family."

The pressure mounted as local party officials visited Aro and made veiled threats. They informed him that the government did not believe a single man could adequately parent a small child and that Hanlee might be removed from his home if he did not quickly find a mother figure for her. Aro had to hide his feelings of dread about the decision he was being forced to make.

In his bed alone at night, he mulled over the horrible choices. *If I don't take a new wife, I will lose my daughter. Once the commissars have made their wishes known, they cannot and will not take them back. I'm trapped! If Sulee hears I'm with another woman she will be devastated.*

She will imagine I've forgotten her. She will lose all hope of being rescued. Can I expect her to understand the predicament I'm in? Would I if the situation were reversed? His mind then turned to his daughter. *My first consideration must be for Hanlee. She has already lost her mother. What would it do to her young mind if she was wrenched away from her father too? I can't do that to her. My decision is made. I have no choice but to obey.*

By month's end Aro married Xin, much to the horror of Uncle Luang. He dreaded having to break the news to Sulee that her husband had a new wife and child. On top of that, Hanlee would now have a new mother.

Dr. Luang spent his time juggling the complicated ruse he had devised for Sulee and the work he so loved in his clinic. His increasing success with fever cases kept him focused. Though he wished no one ill, he knew that the more patients he saw, the greater were his chances to someday vanquish the disease. He began submitting his findings on a possible limited cure for dengue fever to international medical journals. It wasn't until he had cured the son of a local party leader, however, that anyone responded to his claims of success. The doctor had spread the word around many adjacent villages that anyone experiencing the slightest signs of ill health should see him immediately. A local party leader brought his twenty year old son, Yu, for treatment.

At first Luang hesitated. His new patient looked the picture of health! He complained of fatigue, and he had a very slight fever. The doctor could not afford to take a chance with this young man, considering his status. He gave him a strong dose of his latest antidote, a dose which could result in serious side effects. Many of his previous patients experienced severe stomach cramps and vomiting. Some were left weakened after bouts of insomnia and crippling headaches. Luang drew blood from the twenty year old man and, after sending him on his way, he rode all night to the closest lab to have the sample analyzed.

Sure enough, the results were positive for dengue fever. Luang raced back, going straight to the patient's home. Yu was now gravely ill. His blood pressure was weak and his body temperature was dangerously high. He was in and out of consciousness, faintly calling out to his mother for help. Luang stayed by his side. With meticulous attention to his patient's responses, he varied the medicinal dose every few hours. After one week, the symptoms began to subside. Though debilitated and exhausted, Yu's bodily functions slowly returned to normal.

When the danger had clearly passed and the young man was on his way to a full recovery, his father, Comrade Lu, grasped the doctor's hands and kissed them. With tears in his eyes, he confided, "Yu is my only son, so strong, so bright and with so much promise. I have great plans for the boy's future. My gratitude to you, Dr. Luang, can not be expressed strongly enough. If there is ever anything I can do in return, all you need do is ask."

"It has been my great honor to help you, sir." Answered Luang humbly.

Soon after the successful treatment of Yu, Luang was visited by officials of the nearest large city. They encouraged him to work harder and longer and to be bolder in his experimental treatments. Together, the doctor and Xin began to treat and cure more and more early onset cases.

It was during this period of Dr. Luang's frenetic work and increasing success that Sulee gave birth, below ground, to a baby boy. She named him Chan. She ached to share her new son with Aro, who she knew could not take the risk to see her. Although her uncle had explained that her husband's decision to marry was for the sake of their daughter, she took the news badly. Luang held her close to him as she wept, *In one cruel stroke I have lost my husband and my daughter!* How she longed to hold little Hanlee in her arms.

Life was bleak for Sulee. She was disheartened and discouraged. Her thoughts were sullen.

Never did I realize that I might regret the decision to hide myself and my baby from harm.

Never did I imagine that isolation and loneliness could cause so much pain. The one thing Sulee had to hold onto was the hope that her uncle would miraculously find a way to free her.

She never lost faith in him. She sought comfort in her beautiful new baby's love.

Chapter Ten

Gengia family life trudged along uneventfully through James' early and middle childhood years. Sonia grudgingly adapted to her insular existence. She lowered her expectations by degree with every passing year. Gone were the hopes for a rewarding career. With only a high school education and little work experience, she doubted that she would ever amount to anything more than a stay-at-home mother. Her dreams hadn't died but they were now a dim memory. They served only as a reminder that when she had dared to try to find fulfillment and excitement, she had been hurt. She now believed that it was foolhardy to stray beyond the bounds of her home and her immediate family. The opinions Marie had preached over and over had taken root. This dejected mother and daughter were all but paralyzed by fear of the new and unknown. They superstitiously guarded their meager circumstances, believing that any step forward could easily become a false step leading to further hardship. Out of financial necessity, however, Marie began working at the local five and dime. Sometimes, in the busy seasons, Sonia would be called in to help her mother at the checkout counter. She had to admit to herself that she enjoyed occasionally getting out of the house and interacting with people.

She began looking for steadier work but, with little experience and no education beyond high school, it was not to be found. Her days were spent cooking and cleaning in their small apartment while waiting for her mother and James to come home.

Though James grew up in less than ideal conditions, he was usually able to shrug off the dreariness surrounding him. He appeared to be an average child in every way. He wasn't an outstanding student. He wasn't particularly good-looking, though he had an engaging smile and an adorably freckled nose. He had no obvious talents, but his teachers noticed in him a keen curiosity. He was always questioning what he learned, but he kept his opinions to himself so no one knew if he understood the explanations he was given. Despite the less than optimal conditions of his young life, however, James was a very happy boy. In spite of his mother's and grandmother's negativity, it was his nature to look on the bright side. Although he was made well aware, at a very early age, that danger and uncertainty lurked in the unknown, he grew to be a generally optimistic young fellow. Everyday he awoke with the thought that life was full of wonder. He was fascinated by the beauty of his rural surroundings. From his bedroom window he could see a landscape replete with huge fir trees, framed by distant mountains. By his early teens, he had come to anticipate each season and the miraculous changes they would bring to the panorama before him.

James could not reconcile his appreciation of the world around him with the dispositions of his caretakers. After school each day, he walked the four blocks home with anxious anticipation in his heart. School had been fun, he had plenty of friends, but the thought of entering the gloomy apartment and facing the two unhappy women waiting there for him was often too much to bear. He took his time. The big church on the corner offered an excuse to tarry. He loved to drink in the intricate architecture and lovely stained glass windows. He even thought about going inside, but never had the nerve.

On occasion, as he walked home from school, James noticed a strange looking duet in a long gray car pulling up to the curb in front of the church. He would watch them as they slowly exited their vehicle with many grunts and moans. They were two old men. One looked rather plain, tall and thin and stern. The other man had a full, gray beard, gray, bushy hair and wore an odd looking black hat. They both wore long black coats which made them look even skinnier than they were. They would notice James staring at them and they would always make a gesture to acknowledge him. He was very curious about them, but did not make any attempt to discover their purpose or their identities. He had very little contact with adults outside of school and family and was shy to the point of trembling when forced to interact with them.

One day as James walked home, the skies opened up and torrents of rain began to fall. He hadn't taken a jacket to school and he was quickly drenched as he ran ahead, blinded by the driving rain and hail. James was running down the sidewalk when he slammed into the bearded old man. He heard a loud "oomph" and looked down to see that the old man was now lying on the sidewalk, struggling to get up. His friend tried, but couldn't raise him, so James bent down and helped. Together James and the stern-looking man hoisted the third back into the car. They were all sopping wet.

The stern one looked at James and calmly asked, "Will you run into the church and get the Father? Father O'leary is his name. Please hurry!"

James, shaken, but relieved to have been asked to leave the scene, quickly answered, "Yes, I'll be fast!" He ran into the church and immediately started yelling, "Father O'leary! Are you here? Father O'leary!"

Out from his office came an elderly, diminutive, jolly looking priest. "Hello there young man.

Can I help you? What is it you need?"

"Come quick! There's been an accident. Your friends are out front and one of them has fallen. We need your help!"

"Yes, yes. Let's go." He walked with a wobble but he was able to move like lightening when he had to.

The Father stuck his head in the car and asked, "Who's hurt? Is it you, Herman? Did you break anything?"

"No, no. I'm just bruised. Maybe you'd better take me home. I just need to lie down for a bit. Minnie'll fix me up."

The other man chimed in. "A hot bath will do you well. Let's get him home." He turned to James. "Young man, can we impose on you to come with us? We may need help getting him up the stairs to his house."

"Yes, I'll be glad to help," James replied, though in the back of his mind he worried that his mother would be waiting for him at home. He decided he'd deal with that later.

They all piled into the old, gray sedan which smelled musty and felt like a damp cave. Father O'leary turned to James and said in a lilting voice, "You're such a helpful fellow and we don't even know your name!"

"My name is James, James Gengia. I'm in eighth grade at Lincoln Middle School and I live up the street.

"Well, we're glad to have such a fine lad so nearby, in case of emergencies like this! I've noticed you many times walking by the church."

"Yes, every day, to and from school. My grandma likes church, but she doesn't ever go," James stammered. "I've never gone myself!"

"Maybe now that we all know each other, we can change that. You have an open invitation.

You and your grandmother."

"I live with my mother, too."

"Oh, she's very welcome, of course! Bring the whole family."

"It's only the three of us," James said, looking away.

Father O'leary didn't pry. "Whatever the number, you're all invited. I really hope you, at least, will join us often."

With that they drove off to a section of town that was new to James - a brownstone street set off with lovely trees and small flowerbeds. When they reached the injured man's house, the three saviors helped him up the steps and rang the bell. A stout, cheerful woman answered, took one look at the motley crew and gasped. She ushered them all in and they helped the limping man to a well-worn, navy blue velvet sofa. They all collapsed around him, relieved that he was now safe.

"What happened?" demanded the old man's wife.

"Oh Minnie, don't get all excited!" her husband admonished. "I fell in the rain after running into this fine lad on the sidewalk. I'm a little bruised but I'll survive!"

"Listen Herman", she scolded, "don't tell me not to get excited when I see a ragtag bunch of old men hobbling through my door with a freckled kid who looks like he hasn't had a decent meal in years!"

"Oh, ok, calm down. You can take over now and nurse us all back to health!".

"Well that's what I intend to do, starting with a good helping of soup and some wine for you three. I'll get your robe and some towels for your friends so you can all dry up before you catch your death of cold!"

James looked around him and wondered what he was doing with these people in this odd situation. He wasn't frightened at all. He was more in wonderment of the scene. They didn't even know him, nor he them, but he felt oddly comfortable and all the more so by his new companions' good-natured, matter-of-fact reaction to the recent calamity.

"What's your name, bubbela?" Asked Minnie.

"I'm James, ma'am."

"It's nice to meet you, but tell me, does your mother know where you are? Where do you live? How old are you? Who is your father? "It was a question James had avoided his whole young life.

"Minnie, Minnie, stop hectoring the boy! He'll be fine! He'll call his mother and it will all be all right! Calm down!"

"Really? I'll bet she's frantic. Please go and call her right now!" Minnie demanded.

James realized the old lady was right. At least an hour had passed since he was expected home. He went to the phone, but got repeated busy signals. He started to feel uneasy.

Chapter Eleven

With his increasing success toward a cure for dengue fever, Dr. Luang became famous in the medical community of China. His discovery involved a combination of drugs derived from herbs that were locally available but had never been combined before. Years of mixing, remixing and experimenting almost every day of his forty-eight years finally yielded a working formula, but only for adults, and only if the disease was in its earliest stages. The drugs were too strong for children under eighteen years of age. At least that was his cautious opinion. He felt he could never take a chance on hurting a child who was just beginning to show symptoms of illness.

Only one year after their marriage, Aro's new wife, Xin, contracted the fever that had killed so many across China. Luang failed to see the signs of sickness take hold of his nurse. He was totally preoccupied by the inescapable trap he had helped to create for Sulee and her baby. His constant fear for their safety stood in relief to the success he was having in the laboratory and in his clinic. He and Xin worked side by side but he rarely looked at her, certainly never closely.

Unconsciously, he distanced himself from her because she was the daughter of the woman he loved, Mae Ling. But she was the wrong daughter. She wasn't his daughter. He denied to himself that he was pained by her existence and so he treated her with cool detachment. She was like a tool to him, passing needed items in an impersonal way. Xin felt the doctor's aloofness and so she worked silently. It was only when she fainted on the floor next to him that he noticed anything was wrong. It was too late. Xin was very sick, and, after lying down on a cot in the laboratory, she became comatose. Luang was frozen by his feelings of self-reproach and remorse.

My own nurse, the daughter of my lovely Mae Ling, is probably going to die of the disease I am often able to cure. Had I taken the slightest interest in her, I might have been able to help her, maybe save her life. These thoughts quickly dissolved and others rushed in to take their place. He felt himself turning into a monster. He closed the blinds in the laboratory and locked the doors. He had to hide her from the villagers. He knew this would be possible because no one visited for fear of contracting the disease. The illness was mercifully short. Xin was dead by nightfall. Luang summoned Aro.

When Aro arrived, with his daughter and adopted son in tow, he was shocked to see his wife's lifeless body. His instant reaction was to cry. Emotionally spent from all he'd endured in such a short period of time, he could hardly make sense of everything that had happened. Mi, only a year and a half old, sensed that his mother was no longer with him. He looked around and was bewildered, and then, bereft. He began to cry too. Luang reached down and wiped away the boy's tears. He looked at his thumb. It was covered in yellow puss. Aro saw it too. He looked at Luang, first with alarm, and then with guilty thoughts. His eyes went from wide to yearning.

Luang read them and looked down. He felt ashamed for the ideas they were both having.

There was very little doubt that Mi had the disease. Still, there was some question. What if the child had a cold, or one of the many other possible childhood illnesses. Yet Luang had seen the mucous in his yellow-tinged eyes. He felt overwhelmed by the choices before him. Dare he attempt to treat the child with a very

54

low, but dangerous dose of the serum he knew might be life-saving? Should he wait and see what other symptoms developed, possibly missing his chance to stave off death? His mind was muddled by the life or death decisions he was obligated to consider.

The other reason Luang was in conflict was much more tormenting to a man who prided himself on his high moral standards and impeccable reputation. If this child should get sicker and fail to make it through his illness, if he should die, then Chan, his great-nephew, might have a chance at a normal life. The boys were the same age. Mi's parents were dead. Who would look so closely as to notice the difference? Luang wracked his brain. He turned over all the possibilities. He knew this was not a time to waver, but he couldn't decide on the proper course.

He returned Aro's pleading look with a shake of his head. He needed time to make sense of the tragedy of Xin's death and the critical choices he had to make for her son. He walked away from Aro and the children and went home with a heavy head and a heavier heart.

With Luang gone and no one to turn to for consolation, Aro picked up his stepson and hugged him tightly. He had grown to love the little boy. Tears welled up in his eyes, more from shame than anything else. He knew instinctively that it was futile to allow himself to wallow in emotion.

He lived in a culture that made little room for the expression of individual desires and feelings. If he was hurting, he lived in quiet grief. He had seen so much illness and deprivation that he considered himself lucky to be alive. He was also accustomed to doing as he was told. The days of protest were well behind him and everyone in his community. The nightmare Aro and his family lived was testament to the futility of daring to buck authority in their society.

Aro was torn by his growing closeness to Mi and his burning desire to be with his wife and son.

He missed Sulee fiercely. The prospect of being reunited with her and his son was thrilling but the circumstances surrounding the possible reunion were so tragic that he was unable to feel anything but apprehension. For almost two years he had agonized over the results of the decision to place half his family in hiding. Now he could only hope that they might, one day, be able to recreate what they once had. What he didn't realize, however, was that Sulee was bitterly resentful of the fact that he had remarried and begun a new life with Xin and Mi.

Although she had initially agreed with Luang that it would be too risky to bring Aro to her hiding place, even to see his new son, she had an irrational wish that he would find himself unable to bear their separation. Instead she heard nothing from him and so she felt totally abandoned.

Her long, tedious days were spent hoping for someone to miraculously rescue her. They ended in disappointment and despair. Sulee directed her misery toward the one person she felt had let her down, her husband. She had no intention of returning to him or his bed, ever. Her love for him had turned to disenchantment. She also blamed him for replacing her in Hanlee's eyes and heart. Would Hanlee ever again see her as mother? Sulee doubted it. She thought of Xin as her mother. This was the cruelest blow of all. No, there was no going back to her previous life, even if by some miracle she could.

When Luang arrived back at his home, he was greeted by a mail deliverer who appeared quite agitated. He had been waiting and he was on official business. The message he carried had to be delivered or he would have to answer to his superiors. Luang opened an oversized envelope and began to read. He was invited to be the guest speaker at an international medical conference in New York in one week. He sat down, feeling a bit weak in the knees. The letter, written by unnamed Chinese authorities, went on to say that his work had been followed closely over the past several years. Unbeknownst to him, his progress toward a cure for dengue fever was also widely known abroad. The final paragraph informed him that he would be leaving for New York in four days. The end. There were no further instructions. He was stunned.

There was no time to waste. Luang had to speak with Sulee to begin devising a plan for her and Chan's escape. He made sure all was clear and went immediately down to the secret entrance to Sulee's room. He found her napping next to Chan. He thought, *At least down here they're safe from the fever.* He gently woke her. Sulee saw that he was nervous and excited. His eyes were wide and his hands were shaking uncontrollably. She sat up and motioned for him to stay quiet. They walked to the far side of the room. She held her breath as Luang gave details of what had been happening above.

"Listen carefully Sulee. Xin died tonight. She was struck down by the fever. It is possible that her son Mi has also contracted the disease. Though I pray for his health, we must prepare ourselves for the possibility that you and Chan will be leaving this underground prison in the near future."

Luang went on to tell his niece about the government's decision to send him to America for the medical convention. "I will do my best to convince the authorities that I need to bring along my nurse for assistance. Please understand that there are no guarantees. Though I risk giving you false hope, I need you to be alert to the fact that if and when I do come to get you and the baby, we will have to move quickly!"

The beleaguered young mother quickly grasped the possibility of freedom for her and her son, but she was rightfully scared. She dared not ask her uncle for further details of his plan because she feared that she would be wishing for her own good outcome at the expense of others. Luang made it clear that this was most likely their only chance to escape from a life lived in hiding. She knew he was right and she also knew Chan couldn't live like this much longer. He was walking and talking and he wanted to bust out of their underground prison. She often saw him banging on the walls and trying to climb up to the trap door. She wanted this to be over. Sulee was a brave woman. She had already proven that to herself and Luang. She was ready to prove it again.

"Uncle, what about father?"

"I will speak to him next. I already know that he will not stand in our way, but I will make it clear to him that he will almost certainly face repercussions if we are successful."

"I hadn't thought of that. How can we leave him behind to take our punishment? Maybe we should reconsider the whole thing!"

"No Sulee! No second-guessing! Your father has always found a way to survive, even in the darkest times, and he'll do it again. He would die a slow death of grief if he couldn't rescue his daughter and grandson from an underground cell! I need you to find courage, for yourself and for your family. It will be the key to our future. Can you do that?"

Sulee glanced over at the sleeping cherub across the room. She began shivering uncontrollably. "Yes." She turned back to her uncle and saw him as if for the first time.

"Don't you ever get scared Uncle?"

"I do, but I don't let it stop me. I take it as evidence that I still have my wits about me. Then I try to devise strategies as needed."

This explanation made sense to Sulee. With clenched fists and a determined stare, she looked at her uncle and announced, "I am ready!" Together, they once again made a plan.

As the fickleness of chance seemed to grant his family a path for escape, Luang grappled with the emotions one has when given the power of life or death over another human being. He had always prided himself on being a practical man. His ability to keep his heart from intruding on his work had served him well over the years. He had made great strides in his career as a doctor by way of his discretion and caution. Above all he wanted to avoid taking any unnecessary steps which could be viewed as impulsive or ill advised.

Yes, he reaffirmed to himself. *I will continue to follow the prudent path. I cannot risk treating a very young child with medicines formulated for adults. Even if Mi has contracted the fever, it would be foolhardy to try to interfere and possibly cause more harm than good. After all, who am I to deny fate? Who am I, Uncle Luang from a small village in China, to think I should have a say in anyone's destiny?* He repeated these questions over and over until he was convinced that, in this case, he must let nature take its course.

That night Luang had an unsettling dream. He saw himself walking in a desolate area and he came upon a cave. Inside he found a horse tied to a branch. The horse was so sickly and skinny it could barely stand. There were people near the horse. They were also sickly and skinny and their faces were ugly and distorted - marred by pockmarks and scars. They seemed to be in charge of the horse. Luang left them and returned at night with a heaping bowl of noodles which he began feeding the horse, first in secret, and then more and more boldly, until the horse began to neigh and grow strong. The ugly people were mysteriously gone.

The next morning the doctor brought carefully diluted serum vials to Aro's house and began dosing the very sick child. He worked all day and night to save the boy, but Mi did not respond.

He died within twenty-four hours. The emotions flooding the two men witnessing the child's death ran the gamut from grief to remorse. Both questioned whether they had done enough to try to save the child, but, because Aro had merely been a witness to the tragic passing of the boy, it was only Luang who bore self reproach. As he felt himself descend into a mire of blame and contrition, the mental image of his niece and her baby pulled him back to the demands of the moment. He had little time to think. He had to act. He sent his nephew to find Anlee.

The three men decided to use the underground cellar as a burial place for Xin and Mi. Working quietly in the dark of night, they filled the space with dirt until just enough room was left for the hastily built coffins. They gently laid the bodies to rest, offering silent prayers for their safe keeping in the world beyond. As the secret burial came to an end, Aro agonized about his plan to accompany Uncle Luang to America with Sulee, Hanlee and Chan. *How can I leave without explanation to Xin's mother, Mae Ling? How can I not tell her that her daughter and grandson have died? How can I deny them a proper burial? If the plan is successful, everyone will believe that Xin and Mi are on their way to America as part of Luang's entourage.* As hard as it was, Aro put these thoughts out of his mind. He wanted his family back and this overrode any other considerations.

Luang wasted no time ushering Sulee and Chan up from their hiding place to begin preparations for their daring escape. He carried the boy in his arms up the ladder and out into the open air.

Chan, nearly blinded by the never before seen sunlight, looked around, turning his head this way and that, amazed at what was before him. He fixed his gaze on the faraway mountains.

He couldn't avert his eyes from the huge peaks with their gray blue gowns topped off with shimmering white veils. He pointed and squealed, trying to engage his mother in his excitement. Sulee was overwhelmed by the realization that their nightmare of confinement and hiding was now over. She began weeping uncontrollably. She fell to the ground and kissed the dirt. Then she kissed the cuff of her uncles trousers and cried out her thanks to him and to their God.

Chapter Twelve

Hiding with her son in the back room of the smallest of the huts on the grounds of the hospital, Sulee tried to process her feelings about the deaths of Xin and Mi. Her internal dialogue was awash with disbelief and disquiet. *I fear to even breathe a sigh of relief for what has just transpired. Are we really above ground and ready to make our way to America? Am I somehow to blame for the demise of Xin and Mi? I know I had no hand in it but I admit I never prayed for their well being. Will I face retribution some day?* She dared not anticipate the success of her uncle's escape plan. To quiet her nerves, it was necessary to stay in the moment and follow his instructions to the letter.

The day before the scheduled departure to America, Luang gathered his notes. He left a copy of all his work and methods of cure for his colleagues. He sorted through pictures he would bring to show the world photos of the herbs he used in his cures. But he had more than that in mind. He wanted to show them the real thing. He knew it wasn't possible to bring herbs and medicines out of China and into the US. He thought long and hard about this dilemma. He went to the closet and took his mother's metal locket out of his knickknack drawer. He carefully cropped two tiny pictures, one of his mother, one of his father, and worked them into each side of the locket. The fit was awkward, but with a bit more cropping, he got it done. He then placed the locket around his neck, looked up to the heavens and thanked his parents for their inspiration. Now he was ready to go and possibly never come back.

As he and Sulee were locking the medicine cabinets in their final preparations for leaving, Luang glanced out the window and saw a large figure walking toward the clinic. He recognized her immediately. He pulled Sulee into the back room where Chan was sleeping and motioned for her to be quiet. She saw the fear in his eyes. She crouched over Chan and began to tremble. He woke and started to cry. Luang ran out front in the hope of diverting disaster.

"Why Myong," he said as he greeted her. "How nice of you to come all this way to say goodbye.

And I see you have a cake for me. How lovely."

"Please, skip the niceties, Luang. You know why I'm here. After all these years, you're finally flying the coop. You're deserting your village and all the people who depend on you. You know as well as I, you'll never return! I could have forgiven you for rejecting me, all those years ago, but this I will never forgive!"

Luang felt his stomach tighten as she went on.

"I understand you're taking Xin and Mi. This is all very convenient, but I'm no idiot. I've been watching all the goings on in this so-called hospital. I demand to see my niece. I want to ask her in person how she can just up and leave without a proper goodbye to me and to her parents. Where is she? If you don't produce her immediately, I'll know I'm right about everything!"

Luang wasn't above lying for the greater good, but in this case he decided to speak in half truths. "I know what you have sacrificed in the name of love, Myong. I did reject you when we were young, but not because I didn't have strong feelings. I was in love, but, as you knew then and know now, my first love has always been my work." He scowled at her as he continued. "I knew I couldn't give a wife and family the attention they would require, so I chose not to take them on. Neither of us married, as you will note. It is not as if I chose another woman over you.

I chose to devote my life to the science of medicine. It was and always will be my passion.

How could I change my nature? Would you have wanted me to? Would you have loved me if I did? I doubt it. Don't try to avenge your disappointments at this late date!"

"How special it must be to be Dr. Luang!" sneered Myong. You even assume I'm still in love with you! Well that's not why I'm here. You are not what I want. I want to go with you! I want to get out of this godforsaken place! I demand that you take me or I'll turn you all in."

Luang looked at her in disbelief. "And just how do you propose that I explain your need to come along with us? You have no reason to be included in our entourage in the eyes of the authorities."

Myong's devious eyes lit up. "I have a plan! I thought it all through. You'll tell them we have been a secret couple for years and that you cannot be separated from your beloved. Your ability to perform your duties in America will suffer and you refuse to go without me!"

Luang's thoughts raced through his mind. *This horrid woman could ruin everything. I will have to agree in order to shut her up.*

Just then Aro appeared with Hanlee walking beside him. He had a determined look as he walked up to the hut. Myong looked at him derisively. "Your little scheme is out now. I know everything."

Aro was startled. He stared at Luang.

"Don't say a word, Aro," warned Luang. "Let me handle this."

Luang made some quick calculations and finally said, "Well, it looks like we're all going. I hope everyone is ready because here comes the police van to pick us up."

Out of the van walked two officials looking serious and stern. They walked up to Luang.

"Dr. Luang!" shouted the shorter and older of the two. "We're here to take you to the airport.

Is everything in order?"

"There are some changes I need to explain, sir."

"Changes? What changes? There will be no changes!"

"Please let me explain." He told the official about the additional passengers, who they were and why they needed to come along. He explained that he couldn't demonstrate his work without his English speaking nurse, and she wouldn't leave without her husband and children.

Then he told the tale of his lover, Myong. He was very matter-of-fact, but the official was an experienced man who read faces very well.

"What have we here?" the man thought to himself. "It isn't surprising others want to go.

People dream of leaving all the time. The question is, what does Dr. Luang really want?"

"I've made my decision," he announced. "Everyone, except you, Madame, get your bags and get in the van."

Myong stared at him in anger and disbelief. She buried her head in her hands and began to sob. The official approached Myong and put his hand on her shoulder. "I think you know this is best. Your place is here, in your village, with your people. This is not an adventure for a woman like you. You will thank me in the end." Myong nodded in obedience without looking up. More than anything, she wanted to survive. If she dared to reveal all that she knew and suspected she could be accused of abetting a subversive plot. She stood up and left quietly, avoiding all eyes. Luang hoped his feeling of relief wasn't audible or visible. When Sulee was sure the woman was gone, she brought Chan out of the hut. They all piled into the van. Sulee understood that Aro was aching to hold the son he had never before seen. She handed Chan to his father. She wrapped her arms around Hanlee and cooed "I am your mother, my darling."

Chapter Thirteen

The trip to New York went smoothly enough. The children slept most of the way. This gave Sulee and Aro a chance to talk, and talk they did. Using their children as shields on their laps on the way to the airport, they had awkwardly avoided each other's eyes. Their two years apart had left a great gulf between the once blissful couple. The time of reckoning was now before them. Sulee could not help but spill her heart to her husband.

"You look like the man I married, Aro, but I'm not sure you are the same person I once knew and loved. How could I love someone who abandoned me and married another woman? How could I trust the man who handed over my child to a new mother? Did the two of you speak well of me to our daughter? Did you speak of me at all?" she cried. "I was cut to the quick when I realized Hanlee did not recognize me after our years apart. But I wasn't surprised. After all, our little girl was only two years old when I left. She must have been so confused. I'm sure she began to see Xin as her mother. What a cruel blow to be replaced in your child's eyes."

"I never stopped loving you," pleaded Aro. "I longed for you every day and night. My heart was sick." He looked at his wife with longing. "Luang must have explained to you that I also risked losing Hanlee. The local party leaders forced me to remarry or face having our child placed with another family. I couldn't lose her, Sulee. I had to pick from the unwed women. Because none of them mattered in the least to me, I chose the one Hanlee knew as Luang's nurse. I felt this made her somewhat familiar to the child." Aro saw Sullee's look of misery soften. He went on with his

67

explanation. "Xin was never my wife in the way you are thinking. I couldn't touch her or be anything other than formal with her. She wanted more from me, but she never got it. It was always you for me, Sulee, and it always will be. That is why I demanded to be taken along with you. You must believe me! I will proclaim my love until you believe me."

Sulee looked into his eyes and saw his pain. She did believe him but her anger and pride wouldn't allow her to forgive him. Could she tell herself *All's well that ends well?* Not yet. Her heart told her that she was happier than she ever hoped to be, having just escaped, her family intact, her future brighter than before. Her head, however, held onto the ugly facts that had been her life for the preceding two years.

"I want to believe in you again, Aro. I want my hate to turn to love. All that kept me alive underground was my love for you and our children," she said sadly. "When Chan came I was so happy. I thought I could endure anything. Look at him! He has your face, your eyes. When I looked at him I saw you and when I held him I felt you. Then Uncle Luang told me about your marriage to Xin and I thought I would die in my hellhole with a broken heart and broken spirit."

Sulee looked down and lamented, "Chan suffered from my sadness. He tried to comfort me in his sweet little way. I took pity on him and forced myself back to life for his sake. You can't expect me to forgive and forget so quickly. It will have to be earned. Still, I am not sadistic. I don't want you to suffer like I did. I want happiness for our family. I longed for the light when I was in the dark below. Now I will go toward the light but in my own way and at my own pace."

Sulee's tone became stern. "You will have to be patient, Aro. You are lucky that you have two strong allies."

The bruised souls looked at their children, asleep and at peace for the first time in a long while. Aro and Sulee said silent prayers for their future. Sulee fell into a deep, calming sleep.

She dreamt that she was back in her village and she was still in school. She was walking toward the school building, about to enter class. All her friends were there but no one greeted her. They purposely turned away as she walked to her desk. She couldn't understand why she was being shunned. Had she done something to cause such a reaction?

She couldn't remember. She sat at her desk and was afraid to look around. She felt ashamed and alone. She was then with the same friends who were now talking and laughing with her on their way home from school. She didn't know why their moods had changed. She only knew she now felt liked by those around her. She was happy the painful episode had ended. She woke up and tried to recreate the dream and figure out its meaning. Was she worried that she wouldn't have friends in America, that everyone would shun the stranger from China? Yes, she decided, that must be the reason she had such an odd dream.

As the plane ride neared its end, Sulee gave in to an overwhelming desire to mend her marriage and her family. She leaned into Aro's strong shoulder and surreptitiously drank in his smell. She tried in vain to hide how much she longed to melt into his arms. He felt her closeness and experienced a wave of joy. He dared to pray that his wife would relent and take him back into her heart.

Luang had prayers of his own. Once again he would use his wits to secure safety for his fugitive group. He had no doubts, only plans. That was his real genius. It helped him forge ahead where others dared not go. He was rarely trapped by circumstances or convention. The next step was to quietly find a hideaway in the United States. Or maybe not. It occurred to him, after much internal debating, that the best plan for such a group was to openly declare their intention to defect as soon as they arrived. *That's it!* he said to himself. *Think like an American - bold and inherently entitled to freedom. We will become a cause célèbre with supporters scrambling to come to our aid.* This stroke of genius allowed him an escape from the building anxiety he was experiencing with each mile he traveled.

Chapter Fourteen

"Please allow me to introduce myself," Dr. Rozbruch began, "I've been dying to meet you. My name is Sidney Rozbruch. I was the one who submitted your name as the international delegate to our conference."

Luang stepped back and looked at the bespectacled, genial man before him. "How do you do, sir? It is my honor to join your conference. I thank you for your sponsorship."

"The honor is ours! You were chosen because your name is synonymous with independent medical research. While the rest of us in the 'free' world have to work within stringent guidelines and antiquated rules, you've shown yourself to be a sly fox with regard to skirting the zealous control of your government. That may be a bigger story than the actual cure you came up with!

After all, very few in the West contract dengue fever. No, we want to know about you, your methods and your ingenuity."

"I will do my best to provide any knowledge which furthers medical research." Luang answered assuredly.

"The timing of your arrival seems providential because our federal government is just now creating the 'Office of Alternative Medicine' of which I will be a part. I was hoping you might help us with planning and implementation. I know this may be too much to take in at our first meeting and I don't expect an immediate answer. The smile on your face, however, reveals your initial reaction!"

Luang kept his council. He wasn't inclined to give away secrets, but considering his circumstances, he was more than willing to negotiate.

"Dr. Rozbruch, I am your humble servant. I would be glad to help you and I will keep nothing from you, but we will have to speak quickly because I only have three days here."

"Three days? I was sure you'd be staying for a week at least. I'm very disappointed. Is there anything I can do or say to prolong your stay?"

Luang smiled at him, then gave him his most serious stare and said, "I'm so glad you asked."

Dr. Rozbruch took a step back and gulped. "I half expected this, but I must say, I didn't expect it at our first meeting!"

"I do not have the luxury of waiting, I'm afraid. I am here with several members of my family, including two young children. I don't expect you to risk yourself for me, but if you could find it in your heart to connect me with the proper authorities, I would be eternally grateful."

"Yes, yes!" said Rozbruch excitedly. "I'll help you in any way I can. We scientists have to stick together. Where are you staying?"

"We're at a hotel a few streets from here for now."

"No, no. That's unacceptable! I have a large house one half hour from here. You'll all come home with me after the meeting tomorrow. I have to clear it with my wife, but she'll adore having you. She loves intrigue. Our home life has been very dull since the children left. The house is too quiet. We'd love to have you mess it up a bit. How many of you are there?"

"Five, and as I said, two are children."

"Wonderful! I've waited so long to meet you. If you're captive in my house, I'll have more time to pick your brain. Don't worry. I'll keep you busy."

"It is very surprising to find out I have such a good friend who, until today, I never knew existed, Dr. Rozbruch."

"Please, call me Sid."

Luang was an excellent judge of character. He immediately trusted Sid Rozbruch. He felt the family would be safe in his care. Of course, he had no choice but to trust him.

The little group of émigrés was now at the mercy of various American strangers and they were reliant on the American government to take them in. Luang wasn't naive. He knew this could very well turn into an international incident. He hoped Dr. Rozbruch would keep the family's defection as quiet as possible. When he returned to the hotel where the others were sitting in the room, awaiting news of their fate, the calm look on his face told them everything would be all right.

"We are very lucky. America is the good and welcoming place I imagined. The doctor who sponsored our trip is a kind and generous man who has offered to help us. He has even offered to take us into his home. It is good to have faith. I am not often disappointed. Of course, it helps to surround oneself with highly acclaimed scientists whose lives are dedicated to caring for others! We will be safe. We must all resign ourselves to the fact that we will not be going back. Are you both in agreement with that? Please speak up now if you are not."

Aro spoke for himself and his wife. "We are all extremely grateful to be here. There will be no second thoughts, only gratitude and happiness that we put our faith in you, Uncle Luang. We will do whatever you ask to make this work." Sulee, with tears in her eyes, enthusiastically nodded her agreement as the family hugged each other for support.

Having faith in Dr. Rozbruch proved to be a good decision. His wife was at first shocked by his suggestion to take in an entire family. "Sid, you're not serious! You want to bring five people, including two very young children, into our home for an extended period of time? Where will we put them? We only have three bedrooms."

"Not to worry, my dear. Dr. Luang can sleep in my office on a fold away bed. This will only be a temporary situation. They will eventually find their own home I'm sure."

"You're very optimistic, considering they have no jobs, no money, etc."

"We must help them. They are seeking the freedom we take for granted. If you help in this cause you will be doing a good deed, a mitzvah."

That was all her husband needed to say. Helen Rozbruch relished a good cause. She had been on committees and boards for volunteer agencies for many years. She was known as a woman who got things done, no matter the obstacles. Sid was correct in his prediction that she would find the idea of helping political asylum seekers exciting. She immediately went to work on behalf of the emigrating family. She contacted the State Department and reported what had happened. The family was interviewed extensively and finally accepted. They settled in with the Rozbruchs in the suburbs north of New York City. Their transition to America was made with surprising ease thanks mostly to the generosity of the New York couple.

Luang was given a position at the large university hospital where Dr. Rozbruch was chief epidemiologist. He accepted the offer of membership to the Office of Alternative Medicine. Aro found a job refinishing furniture in a local company. Sulee was home with Hanlee and Chan.

Her days were devoted to improving her English and learning how to drive and maneuver in her new surroundings. The children sensed that they were safe, free and part of their rightful family, and so they flourished in their new home. Uncle Luang took time each evening tutoring the children in the language and culture of their native land lest they forget their roots. Hanlee loved his kind attention and quaint rituals. She quickly became his shadow and copied everything he did. Luang sensed that she might one day carry on the healing tradition and so he began to teach her as his father had done with him.

Aro, who had missed the first eighteen months of Chan's life, spent hours watching his son play, marveling at his every move. This was a case of love at first sight. He had a hard time leaving the child for any reason. Chan returned the emotion. The two were inseparable. Although Hanlee was initially taken with her little brother, she quickly came to view him as a rival for her father's attention. Every night she stationed herself on Aro's lap. Hanlee was determined to stay as close to the main attraction as possible. Her father was aware of her need to feel secure in her new surroundings. He knew that she was the one who had experienced the most trauma, first losing her mother, then Zin and Mi. He realized that if he included her in the ritual of observing Chan, she would be assured of her position in the family as the older sibling. They looked on with delight as the toddler made his way from one room to another, here placing a toy in its rightful location; there rearranging what he had just carefully constructed. Chan would squeal with laughter when he discovered something new, causing everyone near him to stop what they were doing and witness his genius. Both children were healthy and rosy cheeked.

Their smiles radiated throughout the household. Their hosts loved having them, though the constant tumult caused by the invasion of a family had turned their lives upside down.

Everyone knew this would not be a permanent arrangement, but for the time being, all were content.

Sid Rozbruch devoted many evenings with Luang discussing his methods of cure and the medicines he had created. When Luang felt thoroughly comfortable with the American doctor, he decided to reveal that he had smuggled his precious seeds into the country. He looked searchingly into Sid's eyes and said shyly, "I have something I've been wanting to show you, something I secretly brought with me from China. It was probably against the law to do so.

Therefore, I must have your solemn promise that you will keep this confidentially between us. I would not want my family to come into any trouble because of my poor judgment."

"Of course I'll keep your secret." Sid answered with anticipation. "I assume anything you've done is for the benefit of science."

"Yes, only for that benefit." Luang went to his room and came back with what looked like an empty jar. Upon closer inspection, Sid saw the jar contained tiny seeds.

"I must explain the significance of what I have here. These are the seeds of an ancient culture.

I'm not sure you can understand their value because you are the product of a new culture."

Dr. Rozbruch demurred. "I beg to differ, doctor. There is no practicing Jew who considers himself belonging to a new culture.

Our origins date back at least as far as yours. This, for us, is the year 5751!"

"I stand corrected. How ignorant of me! I guess we all tend to overestimate the importance of our origins."

"No offense taken. But tell me, how did you get the seeds through customs?"

"Ah, that was ingenious, if I do say so myself. I hid them in a locket behind pictures of my parents."

"Very cunning!" Both men gazed at the seeds with deep reverence. "Now I want to know what they are and how you use them."

"All in good time. I intend to plant them in your garden. When we have some herbs, I'll show you how they're used. I brought all my notes. This was prescient considering your country's new interest in alternative cures."

"Yes, but the soil, the climate! They may not grow here."

"The climate is of little concern. These herbs grow quickly. The soil, however, may be a problem but not one that we can't overcome."

"Your spirit is infectious Luang! I'm so glad you landed on my doorstep."

"It has been mutually beneficial, my friend."

PART TWO

Chapter Fifteen

"Five minutes to air!" The producer's warning shrieked into Sonia's ears. She took a moment to adjust her posture. She checked her face on the screen above her and liked what she saw - a polished woman with the self-confidence of a true media professional. She was making her way in the world of TV news, having started in the time-tested domain of weather reporting.

She had proved to her employers that she had the poise and correctness of manner to come across as believable and likable on camera. They gave her occasional fill-in spots and she performed impeccably. She was on her way.

Sonia mused, *How did I get here? It's still seems like a dream. How did this happen? Did I make it happen or was it fate?* She remembered back to the day her life seemed to take a major turn. At the time, she had no idea it would be a turn for the better. In fact it seemed like her persistent bad luck would never end.

It had been more than five years since the fateful episode when James, only thirteen years old at the time, failed to come home after school. Sonia had been daydreaming while ironing the week's laundry when she heard the pit pat of rain and hail outside the window in the next room.

She realized James would be on his way home wearing only a flimsy shirt and light trousers.

She grabbed her coat and his jacket and bolted out of the house to intercept him.

Running down the street and around the corner toward the school, Sonia saw the other children walking, then sprinting toward their homes. She was sure she would run into James. As she passed the church, she noticed a big gray sedan pulling away from the curb. For some reason, it caught her attention, but she couldn't see inside. She reached the school, hurried in, and headed for James' classroom, but, no James. She walked up and down the corridors, asking every passer-by if they had seen him. A few said they saw him leave more than twenty minutes earlier. She went to his locker and saw that it was empty. She stopped at the school office to call her mother. Maybe James had come home. He hadn't. Sonia began to panic. She felt tears streaming down her face as she ran into the principle's office and breathlessly announced, "James is missing!"

After searching the neighborhood, to no avail, with the principal in his car, they decided they had no choice but to call the police. It was another agonizing hour before James called his house and told his grandmother where he was. Sonia was still searching with the police, school personnel and now, neighbors. When she called home again to see if he had arrived, the news that he was safe was too much for Sonia. She fainted dead away on the floor of the school office.

Sonia was taken by ambulance to the hospital. She had hit her head as she fell and had a serious concussion. She would have to stay overnight for observation. The strong drugs she was given put her in a deep sleep. When she awoke, she was surrounded by five people, only two of whom she knew. There was James, holding a wilting red rose. Her mother was next to him, looking tired and anxious, wringing her hands. But who were the three old men? She thought she was dreaming or imagining she was in heaven and these were the three disciples of St. Peter. In the midst of her hallucination, James sat down on the bed. He lifted her hand and kissed it, tears in his eyes.

"Mother, are you alright?"

"James! I thought I lost you!" She exclaimed. "I looked all over. I thought you were gone, kidnapped, or worse. Then Gramma told me you were okay and everything went dark. Where were you? Who are these people! What happened! No, don't tell me. I know its bad!"

"Mom, Mom, its alright. I met these men. There was an accident. One of them fell and I helped him home. That's all! I promise!"

"It's true Mrs. Gengia," injected the elderly, bearded man. "Your son was a hero yesterday, in a manner of speaking. He helped an old man, me, and I will be eternally grateful. The whole thing happened so fast, we lost ourselves and neglected our duty to stop at your house and ask your permission to allow James to help me home. It's all my fault and I will never forgive myself, but I hope and pray you will forgive James and then, maybe, me."

Rabbi Gellerman looked down at the floor. He felt enormous guilt for having been so selfish the day before. He chastised himself. *My foolhardiness and arrogance has caused this. I shouldn't even be allowed out on the streets. Look what has come of my thoughtlessness! She could have died. I am going to make this up to her if I can.*

Father O'leary patted Sonia's hand. "There, there dear. You've raised a fine boy. I say! As I stand here the color is coming back to your face! Why, you'll be better in no time!"

Reverend Brown finally spoke up. "Madame, allow me to make proper introductions. I am Reverend Nicholas Brown. This is Father O'leary of St. Bartholomew's church, and this is Rabbi Gellerman. We were on our way to our weekly meeting at St.

Bart's yesterday when, blinded by the rain, James and the Rabbi collided on the sidewalk. We needed his help to bring Rabbi Gellerman home and he graciously came along. We were all remiss in not informing you."

As Reverend Brown spoke, Sonia began to feel a deep sense of relief. His soft, soothing voice calmed her. She felt warm and she began to relax back onto her pillow. Her mother had a stronger reaction. Marie couldn't take her eyes off the tall, lanky man. She imagined this must have been what Abe Lincoln had looked and sounded like. He seemed like a gentle giant whose authority emanated from within. She hadn't felt such a strong attraction to a man in many years. She smiled at him and basked in his glow.

James looked at his mother and forced his tears away. She seemed so helpless in her hospital bed. He wanted to protect her. The feeling overwhelmed him. "Mother, I will help you recover and I won't scare you again."

James felt a certain strength in his body as he made this promise. Sonia also noticed a change in his voice and demeanor. All of a sudden he was older, more sure of himself. As he stood up he felt as though, in the blink of an eye, he had grown several inches. Was this the result of his decision to command the situation? He wasn't sure, but the one thing he knew was that he was no longer a little boy.

In the ensuing weeks, the three clergymen stopped in many times at the Gengia household.

Sometimes Rabbi Gellerman visited alone, waiting for James to come home from school. Side by side, they would watch whatever sports were being televised in the family living room.

Hours were spent poring over James' collections of baseball cards, coins and comic books.

Reverend Brown made private calls on the family as well. He would always announce that he was in the neighborhood on church business. Somehow he would end up staying for dinner, taking time in the kitchen to talk with Marie. She was delighted and seemed to come alive as never before.

Every Friday, the Rabbi invited James and his family for Sabbath dinner. Minnie was so warm and motherly with her constant urging to "eat, eat". Grandma Marie started to gain weight and color in her previously gaunt cheeks. It was obvious to anyone who looked that she now appeared to have a blushing bride look. She and Sonia were anxious to contribute to the dinners by cooking up their own favorite dishes of stewed meats and candied cakes. They were disconcerted that their carefully prepared delicacies were never served. In fact, the food never made it into the kitchen, being carefully placed on a table on the screened porch. Minnie thanked them profusely and then quietly slipped away with the never opened bundles of food.

She couldn't bring herself to broach the subject that was on everyone's mind. Finally Marie asked the rabbi, "Why are you not serving the food we brought?"

Rabbi Gellerman looked at her and apologized. "We should have explained to you the first time you came to Shabbat dinner that we observe strict dietary laws. Everything we eat must be 'kosher'. That means that we buy only food which has been verified by a rabbi as having been procured in a certain way and then blessed. We are forbidden to combine milk and meat. We are forbidden to eat pork products and those of certain other animals. I was reluctant to bring up this subject because the rules are very complicated and I didn't want to burden you with our needs. But this was a mistake because I ended up insulting you by not serving your generous gifts. Please forgive me for this error."

"I had no idea. I'm so glad you explained. You can't imagine how relieved I am to know that I may still consider myself a good cook! I've been subjecting Reverend Brown to my meals for several weeks, you know."

"Yes, and he's looking very well nourished lately. In fact I've noticed that you both have a healthy glow! Can I assume, then, that all is forgiven?"

Sonia interjected, "There is nothing to forgive! Please feel free to share what you need to share with me and my family. There is much we need to learn and you are an excellent teacher, especially to James." She said these words emphatically, while looking directly into the rabbi's eyes, as though she wanted him to infer a deep meaning from her words.

"I will do my best," he replied tentatively, unsure if he had just been scolded or newly taken into this woman's dearly held confidence.

Sonia was enjoying her new friends and all the socializing. The mood in her family had lifted because she had opened her home and her heart. She began to realize that she had never before looked to people for comfort and pleasure. She had never encouraged friendships, believing they were more trouble than good. But these were the perfect first friends - old, religious men - completely harmless and well-meaning.

This was the beginning of a new chapter in the Gengia family history. It was hard to imagine so much good coming from a young boy's act of kindness. James took all this in stride. He began to feel close to the elderly gentlemen who befriended him, dropping in at the church every wednesday for their weekly bible discussion. He knew he had a lot to learn and they were eager to teach him what they could.

All three men, it seemed, felt somewhat sidelined in their congregations. They were old, and younger men had been brought in to supplement their work. While they appreciated the help, they missed their positions of power and honor. James gave new meaning to their lives as teachers and inspirational leaders. He was such an apt student. He had never been exposed to religious teachings, even his own. He questioned everything they said, not to challenge them, but to go further and deeper into the meanings in the biblical stories.

Chapter Sixteen

One warm, spring, Friday evening, the Gengia's were preparing to head over to the Gellerman's home for their usual Sabbath dinner. Sonia pondered what would be an appropriate gift for Minnie now that food was out of the question. She decided on a colorful apron and spent days sewing appliqués on the soft lavender and blue cotton garment.

As she carefully folded and wrapped the gift, James strolled into the kitchen and announced that he was not going to Sabbath dinner because he wanted to go to the movies with his friends. He was fourteen years old, after all, and his small group of peers was beginning to turn their attention to girls, parties and any activities which allowed them to spend time together outside their homes and away from their parents.

Sonia called the Gellermans and told them there would be one less for dinner. Minnie started to tell her something about the number of guests when James came back into the kitchen with tears in his eyes. She hung up quickly.

"I'm not going to the movies!" James cried to his mother. My friends say there isn't room for me. They only have room for six and I would be the seventh, so I can't go." He sat down at the kitchen table and stared into space. "They hate me I guess. I hate them too! I'll never go out with them again. I don't even want to see them at school."

Sonia was shocked to hear such a vehement reaction from her mild mannered son. She approached him tentatively and put her hands on his shoulders. She felt his tension and tried to soothe him. He looked at her with wide, moist eyes, as if to say he too was surprised and frightened by his despair.

"Come with us," Sonia begged. "You know you always enjoy Sabbath dinner. Everyone there loves you! They will be so disappointed if you're not there. I won't go without you, James.

Neither will Grandma."

James calmed himself, turned on his heels and went to his room to get ready. He wasn't sure why he was so distraught about being slighted by friends who were typically immature and insensitive. He only knew that he felt a deep hurt and he was not looking forward to forcing himself to be sociable at the Gellerman's. He didn't want to go but neither did he want to ruin his family's evening. They weren't to blame. He told himself there would have to be some changes made, and soon. Maybe some new activities, maybe some new friends. He didn't want to be in this situation ever again.

The family, all feeling sad and dreary, left for the Gellerman's. Living together in such close quarters for so many years made them acutely sensitive to each other's emotions. When they arrived, Minnie met them at the door and immediately registered their low spirits. She took a look at James, saw that he was on the verge of tears, and knew something was wrong. She cradled him into her warm, chubby body, kissed him on the cheek and said, "Oh Bubbela, my Jamesela, I'm so glad you decided to come! What would our Shabbat be without you? You make it all fun. And besides, we will have surprise guests for you to meet. Come in, come in!

You all look so nice."

James kissed her back and smiled. They all went inside the

Gellerman's house and made themselves at home. James realized he was beginning to love this little old woman with her kind, watery eyes. At least he felt as comfortable in her home as he could feel anywhere in the world.

Chapter Seventeen

"Mom, Dad, we're here!" shouted a man from the front door.

That voice! James felt his heart begin to thump. He had a funny feeling in his stomach. Yes, he knew that voice. That was the voice of the man who had called him twice a year for at least the last five years, the man who cryptically asked questions about his life without ever revealing much about himself. He'd always say he was a family friend, but James was leery. He knew his mother was aware of the calls but they went carefully unmentioned.

James sat motionless on the sofa, trying to sink in so deep he would disappear. Before he could, a tall, well-built man strolled happily into the room with a young boy and two adorable, curly haired tots. They were twins, dressed alike, about two years old. James didn't know where to look first. He was relieved that the man brought along distractions. Sonia walked into the room next, carrying a tray of food. She stopped dead in her tracks and stared at the new arrivals. She recognized Mark instantly. She looked at James and saw that he was confused.

Now what? she thought. *Will Mark recognize me?*

He did. "Sonia! Is that you? After all these years! What are you doing here, I mean, how nice to see you!" His face went pale as he looked at the teenaged boy on the sofa. "Who's this young man?" he asked almost breathlessly.

"This is James, my son."

"Oh. So nice to meet you," he gasped.

James didn't know what to say. He looked at the children. Finally, he asked, "Are these your kids?"

"Yes, this is Sam. The twins are Dina and Eliana."

Mark was now at a loss. He couldn't take his eyes off James. The resemblance was uncanny. James even had his freckled nose! As the room filled with angst and high emotion, in bolted Minnie with a bell dangling between her fingers. She beamed as she modeled the colorful apron Sonia had given her.

"Dinner is served!" she bellowed, ringing the bell for effect. Everyone quickly made their way into the dining room and sat through an enormous meal beginning with soup and ending with cake. Somewhere between courses, Mark managed to slip a note to Sonia. She read it and caught his eye. "Yes", she nodded. "I will call you tonight."

As soon as he could do so politely, Mark excused himself and the children saying they had a long ride back to the city where his wife would be awaiting them. Everyone kissed goodby, and off they went. Sonia, Marie and James stayed behind and helped clean up. Sonia tried to remain calm, but she could barely contain her nerves. She knew that Herman and Minnie had no idea of her connection to Mark, although they were both uncharacteristically quiet all day. They were quick to pick up vibes, and the current was higher than usual among all their guests.

Later that night, as Minnie was cleaning the kitchen, Herman walked in the room and asked, "Is everything alright?"

"What do you mean?" she responded, as she looked at him closely to see if she could read his mind through his eyes.

"I was just wondering if you're alright."

"Herman, I have a funny feeling about what happened tonight. I don't know what was going on but I felt like there was a secret everyone but us knew."

"Don't be so dramatic Minnie! You're imagining things."

"Oh really? Then why did you come in here asking if I'm alright?"

"I just didn't know that Mark knew Sonia. Did you?"

"No, I didn't. And I didn't know that James knew Mark either."

"What?"

"Oh yes. James recognized him somehow. I'm sure of it."

"Now you're being ridiculous," he said dismissively as he turned to walk away. He stopped and looked at his wife. "You think so?"

"Do you?"

"I don't know what to think! Maybe we should just stay out of it."

"I can't stop wondering about it. I'm scared and excited at the same time."

"Stop wondering Minnie. Stop getting excited. Why don't you just worry like me?"

"It's the boy you're worrying about."

"I guess it is."

They went to bed. Herman dreamt he was driving a fast car. The brakes weren't working well. He couldn't slow down. Just when he was sure he would crash, a huge, beautiful bird landed on the roof and spread its wings, slowing the car and bringing it to a halt. Minnie, who couldn't sleep, heard him grunting and moaning all night.

Chapter Eighteen

Mark answered his phone. "Sonia, we need to talk in person. Will you meet me tomorrow?"

"Yes, we must talk as soon as possible. Can you come to St. Bartholomew's church in the morning? It's a few blocks from your parents' home. Do you remember? I'll ask Father O'leary if we can use one of his private offices."

"I know where it is. That's a good idea. I'll see you there at 10 A.M?

As she hung up the phone, James walked into her bedroom.

"Mom, I'm so confused. I don't even know what I'm confused about. That man, Mark. Who is he? I mean, I know he's Minnie and Herman's son, but who is he? I think he's been calling me for years, asking how I am, if I need anything. I never told you because I didn't want to upset you. It was him. I recognized his voice as soon as he spoke. And why do I look exactly like him? Mom?"

James was in tears. Sonia also welled up and motioned for him to come to her. She clasped her son to her and said, "I'm sorry. I'm so sorry I never told you about your father."

"No, I don't believe you!" James cried out. "It can't be! That means Herman and Minnie are my grandparents? Mom! It can't be!" James was near hysterics. He was sobbing into his mother's shoulder. "Did you know that? Did you know that all along?"

"When I saw all of you that day in the hospital, I was too confused and upset to realize who Rabbi Gellerman was. After everyone left, I kept thinking about that name, Gellerman. Mark and I had been close friends in high school." As soon as she said that, Sonia realized she was not being entirely truthful. "It was more than that, really. He was my boyfriend for most of our senior year. We thought we were in love and I pictured us getting married." She looked at James to see if he understood, but his face was blank. She decided to go on with her explanation anyway.

"I knew Mark's father was religious. He had told me that we could never be a real couple because I wasn't Jewish and his parents would never accept me. I didn't know for sure that his father was a rabbi. When I got out of the hospital, I made some inquiries. After that, yes, I knew the Gellermans were your grandparents." Sonia's voice became tearful and plaintive as she relived the months leading up to this day. "I've thought about nothing else since. That was why I opened the door to our lives to them. I wanted to tell you but I didn't know how. You were so happy together. It was as if you all knew without knowing. I didn't want to ruin it.

I knew this day would come and I dreaded it," she sobbed. I've made mistake after mistake, but through it all I only wanted what was best for you, James." Sonia gathered herself, sat up straight, and in a serious tone she said, "Grandma and I have very few resources. There isn't a lot we can do for you. Soon you'll be a young man. I know I can't give you the life you deserve to have. It was a godsend to me when your grandparents came into our lives. For whatever reason, we cut ourselves off from our neighbors and our community. We've just been the three of us and I now realize that isn't enough. Now there's a chance you'll finally know your father. A boy needs his father," she added pleadingly. "As upsetting as everything seems, can you try to find anything good coming out of it? It may be too soon to ask you to do that. I won't push you. I know you need time to sort this out."

Mother and son were crying softly. They separated slowly and James went to his room. He wanted to be alone. He wanted quiet. He didn't want to think anymore. He just wanted to lie on his bed and stare at the ceiling. After a while, Marie looked in on him. He reached out for her and began to sob again. "Look on the bright side," she said as she comforted him in her arms. "Your family has just doubled in size! And, lo and behold, your new grandparents are people you already know and love! Really James, could there be a happier ending?"

Her grandson was unable to respond. He was still shocked by what he had just learned.

Nothing Marie said could lessen his anguish at that moment. He felt betrayed by everyone he held dear. He wondered if they would ever have granted him the opportunity to meet his father had it not happened by chance. The ache in his heart was overwhelming. He tried not to imagine all that he had missed over the years.

When Marie left his room, James curled up in his bed, closed his eyes and fell into a deep sleep. In a dream that seemed surreal, he was swimming in dark ocean waters. Somehow, a great whale came up beside him. He climbed onto the whale's back. He felt exhilarated.

He felt completely safe. He felt they could swim as far as they wanted together. When he woke up the next morning, his legs were weak. It was a while before he could find the strength to walk.

Chapter Nineteen

The next day, after a sleepless night for both, Mark and Sonia met outside the church. They entered and were greeted by Father O'leary who granted their request to speak in a private room. As they sat down to talk, Mark noticed Sonia was trembling.

"Are you all right?" he asked.

"I have so many thoughts running through my mind," she replied. "I'm having a hard time calming down. I told James everything last night. He was sobbing uncontrollably. Then he stayed quietly alone in his room. This morning his mood was changed. He seemed happy! He was avoiding me, but he actually joked with my mother. I don't know what to make of his turnaround."

"Don't question it. Just be thankful. Maybe he's relieved that life isn't such a mystery anymore. Whatever the reason, let's not delve too deeply and remind him he ought to be very upset!" "Yes, I guess you're right."

"Sonia, the first thing I want to do is apologize for so many things that I don't know where to start. If you'll accept my blanket apology, I want to move on and discuss other pressing issues I've been considering."

"Go on," Sonia said cautiously. She didn't see any reason to grant forgiveness for what was now ancient history. Neither did she want to absolve herself or Mark for the pain they caused their son.

"Well, to begin with, I was hoping you would accept my help. I don't want to overstep my bounds in your family's life, but I do want to meet with James. I want to start some type of relationship with him if he'll let me. I want to be there for him and for you in any way I can."

"The truth is, "Sonia interjected, "your parents have already helped James, my mother and me more than you know. We were all so lonely and isolated before they came into our lives.

That's the reason, I think, that James is smiling today. He found out his adopted grandparents are his grandparents in reality! By the way, have you told them? They'll be floored. I must say, my mother has taken it all in stride. She's preoccupied, I guess."

"No, I haven't told them. This news will come as a shock to them, I'm sure, but months ago they told me that they intended to adopt a young boy and his mother and grandmother into their family. I didn't take their intentions seriously. I didn't even ask much about the family they were so enthralled by. I had no idea it was you! My father, especially, is on a mission when it comes to you and James. It hit him hard when he saw you in the hospital. He blamed himself for your injuries. Once he got to know you all better, he couldn't get enough of you. My mother feels the same. I think it's been a very good thing for all. My wife and I are so busy with work and the children that we can't visit upstate as often as we'd like. You and James have filled a void for my parents. You've made them feel valued and needed . From what you tell me, they've provided you with some much appreciated love and attention. The relationship has been a blessing all the way around.

Now I want to talk about what I can do for James. I've been very lucky these past several years. I married a wonderful woman, Ruth. I have to admit that I worship her because she's the kindest and fairest person I know, next to my mother, of course. We talked all night. She is behind me every step of the way. She truly wants the best outcome for everyone. I really don't deserve such mercy, but that's beside the point. Ruth knows that our kids are the light of my life. We haven't even planned their futures yet, but time is of the essence with James. He's headed for high school, right?"

"Yes. He's in eighth grade. Not the best student, but not the worst either. What do you mean, time is of the essence?"

"Well, I was thinking. Maybe he'd get a better education in private school, prep school, I mean."

While Sonia and Mark spent hours discussing their son's future, James was at home trying to piece together his past. Not only did he have to navigate the storm of adolescence and the disappointments he constantly faced with his small group of friends, now he had to figure out his own identity. He remembered wondering, at a young age, where his father was. He couldn't recall if he ever asked his mother, but somehow she let him know that she didn't want him to put her through the pain of explaining the origins of his birth. He complied. He scrupulously avoided the topic, even in his own mind. Now, out of the blue, all the questions and answers were colliding. His brain felt like it was on a high-speed roller coaster. In a way it was exciting but he also wanted it to end so that he could feel he was standing on solid ground again.

There were too many possible dangers, some that he could see clearly and some he sensed were lurking. He didn't know where his place was in his newly discovered father's family. Would his father want to see him again? What about his new half siblings? Would they all live together? And what about the fact that he was half Jewish? What did that mean exactly? It was all too much for a teenage boy to sort out. As he tried to consider each question, he became overwhelmed and put them out of his thoughts. They refused to stay out, however, and he felt tormented and confused.

Finally, after waiting most of the day for his mother to return and answer all that was on his mind, James decided to focus on the one positive thought that kept bubbling to the surface. Herman and Minnie were his grandparents. He felt safe with them and he knew that his new status wouldn't change their feelings toward him. He left his house and walked to theirs.

Chapter Twenty

The Kahn family quickly adapted to their new home. Hanlee was initially reluctant to allow Sulee to embrace her and treat her as her child. The four year old girl often ran to her father rather than succumb to her mother's hugs and kisses. Aro eased the tension by pretending to be preoccupied. This left his daughter no choice but to seek out her mother for care. It wasn't long before his strategy worked. Sulee thanked him for helping to bring the child back to her arms.

"I've waited a long time to hear my baby girl say, 'I love you, too.' Last night, when I put the children to bed, she did just that! I know it was your encouragement that helped end Hanlee's hesitation to accept my affection. Now, after our long ordeal, we are a proper family again."

"We accomplished this together, my darling." Aro said lovingly. "It was you who suffered most.

Hanlee knows in her heart that only her true mother would make any sacrifice necessary to keep her children safe."

Sulee drank in his words and decided to begin to distance herself from the pain of her ordeal. "I must now focus on moving forward. The time for grieving and soothing old wounds is over.

There is much we can accomplish for ourselves and our children in our new country. We are blessed to have this opportunity. We cannot waste it by looking back with regrets."

"Your words are like a soothing balm for my soul, Sulee."

With that they both considered the subject of the past closed.

Having lived with their hosts for almost two years, the family realized it was time to find a place of their own. They chose to stay nearby, renting a small house a few blocks from the Rozbruchs'. Luang could not bear the thought of putting too much distance between him and his dearest friend Sid.

Chan quickly overtook his big sister in size. He learned English as his first language and so he was the most proficient in his family. They looked to him for explanation and proper pronunciation. He, being the youngest, loved his position as teacher to all his elders. It made him feel important and useful. His family relied on him, as the years went by, to guide them in their adopted country. Chan was an adept teacher. The logical outcome for the child was that he loved school. To the delight of his learned uncle, he excelled at every grade level. The proud family cried with joy when he consistently won top honors in public school. His achievements did not go unnoticed by the Rozbruchs. They suggested that he apply for scholarships to preparatory schools in the area. Hanlee had been offered the same chance but turned it down. She had no desire to live apart from her loved ones. The young teenaged girl cherished her family. She considered her father her "rock", the one she relied on to make her feel secure. Her mother was the heart of the clan. Her warmth and patience made their home a haven from the mundane world. Uncle Luang rounded out the group. He was always available to offer encouragement. He saw great potential in both children, but it was to Hanlee that he looked for the perpetuation of the healing tradition begun by their ancestors. The interest she showed in his work at the hospital and in his thriving herb garden made the promise of a career in medicine seem very possible for his grandniece.

The idea of going to a boarding school and making his way on his own excited Chan. He agreed to the plan without hesitation. His parents were amazed and somewhat dismayed at the ease with which he contemplated leaving them. They reluctantly consented, knowing their son deserved the rare chance to further his talents in an elite school.

Because of Chan's academic superiority and his status as a foreign born student, he was accepted to many of the schools with a guarantee of paid tuition. After visiting all of them, he and his parents chose the one closest to home. Family always came first. Aro, especially, dreaded the day when he could no longer wake up and see his son. He would miss him at breakfast, when the Khans discussed their plans for the day. He would miss their nightly talks about events that had occurred and their dreams for the future. Most of all, he would miss kissing him goodnight, a ritual they both held onto longer than most fathers and sons.

As the day of his Chan's departure drew near, the family became quiet and glum. No one knew exactly what to expect. What would daily life be like without their beloved Chan? They couldn't even talk about it. Sulee approached Aro with her usual courage. "So, are we all going to act like there's been a death in the family from now on? Or can we please dig deep into our feelings and find some excitement for our son's new adventure? It would be selfish not to cheer him on before he goes. That's the least we, as his parents, can do. He has done so much for us. Do you agree?"

"Of course I agree, but it's easier said than done. I know I'm selfish, but I don't want him to leave," admitted Aro. He put his arms around his wife and held on tightly, as if to say, "As long as I have you, I can get through this." She looked at him and nodded reassuringly. This gesture enabled him to put on the best face he could muster, as he had always done for his loved ones. The family spent weeks helping Chan pack and prepare to leave. He showed no signs of fear. Although he had regrets about leaving all that he knew behind, he felt an overwhelming urge from somewhere deep inside to break out of the confinement of hearth and home and make his way in the world.

Chapter Twenty-One

During the spring and summer before his freshman year in high school, James spent all his free time lifting weights and bulking up his body. He joined every sport team he could and attended practice almost every day. This was the first step toward his plan to make new friends and change his previously sheltered life. His body responded by busting out in all directions. He grew several inches and gained almost twenty pounds.

Sonia and Marie witnessed this quick transformation and were amazed. Mark was also struck that the son he had just recently met was becoming a hulking young man. Sonia had confided that their boy had often felt let down by his small circle of friends and had decided to make an effort to expand his interests and his social life. Mark saw this new beginning as an opportunity to step in and try to make it a father-son project. He drove upstate whenever he could and coached James during his after school games. He joined his son at the gym for workouts. It became a pleasant routine for both. The hours spent together helped them build a relationship.

When he felt he and James had become familiar enough to talk about his future, Mark approached the boy with the idea he had discussed with Sonia.

"James, would you ever consider private high school?"

"Why? What's wrong with my school?" he asked cautiously, always suspicious that there might be something he should know.

"Nothing. It's just that the right prep school would offer you a far better education and more opportunities. I know this is a new idea and you may not even know much about these schools.

You live at them. They're boarding schools. You only come home on holidays and, of course, summers."

"That sounds terrible! Even though I'm not thrilled with my friends right now, I don't think I'd want to leave them. I've known them all my life. Besides, I'm doing so well at all my sports. I'd hate to let the teams down. They rely on me because I'm the biggest, not to mention the fastest!" He spoke with pride about his newfound status.

"While I certainly agree that you are needed on your teams, I'm hoping you'll consider the idea that high school is a time of new beginnings and new opportunities, especially for someone with your strengths and talents. I'd like to see you expand your horizons beyond what is familiar to you right now. You would be an asset to the team at any school you attended. Would you at least be willing to look at a few academies with me and your mother?"

James tried to make his father understand that he was not interested without overtly saying so.

He didn't want to do or say anything to upset their growing bond.

"When? I have very little free time now."

His father wasn't easily dissuaded. "Let's find a day to take you around to visit some campuses.

All I ask is that you keep an open mind. The final decision is up to you."

"Okay, I guess." James replied with hesitation. His strong reluctance toward change had been instilled from birth. At the same time, he had to admit to himself that his life had been made richer and fuller by his willingness to accommodate new experiences. He decided to consider his father's idea, but he had every intention of rejecting it in the end.

The lukewarm reply was the opening Mark needed to encourage his son out of the nest. The wheels were now in motion. As with all his plans, Mark was a man on a mission. He wanted James to see more of the world than the backwater town where he had spent his own childhood. He also wanted James nearer to him so that they could build on the closeness they were beginning to feel. He took his son and Sonia on a tour of three fancy campuses, dazzling the boy and his mother with beautiful quadrangles, enticing dining rooms and colossal gymnasiums. James imagined himself playing football in a real stadium. He fantasized about the sense of freedom prep school would give him. He felt himself embracing the idea of moving on to a new episode in his life. He began to understand that he could not turn down the good fortune that had come his way.

Mark assured Sonia that she would be included in the plan. He promised to help her find work and lodging in the city so that she could be near her son. He explained that he had friends and colleagues who would help her get started in a career in broadcasting if this was still her interest. Sonia cautiously sensed her luck changing. She trusted Mark and his motives. She believed the many changes they were about make would benefit her family, especially her son. Though it was a new feeling, she liked the idea of having hope for the future. It was a moment of awakening for her when she realized that James was warming to the idea that he could feel safe and comfortable in one of the grand enclaves they'd visited. She began to let herself consider the possibility that a brighter future for her family may lie ahead.

Chapter Twenty-Two

All those close to James held their breath as they awaited the decision from the school he had chosen. There was jubilation when the acceptance letter finally came. The encouragement he had from family and friends gave him the confidence he needed to overcome any lingering fear he had about succeeding in his new endeavor.

Move-in day came. James was packed and ready to go. Everyone in his circle wanted to accompany him to his school. A small caravan of cars, led by Mark, headed south. As he drove out of town, James passed the church and then the high school. He felt a pang of regret that he had decided to leave. He felt he was giving up everything and everybody he had forever known. There were so many changes to keep track of. His mother was also moving to be close to him. He wondered if she truly wanted to leave her mother's home. He considered that Grandma Marie was in the midst of her own life decisions. She was thoroughly preoccupied with her new love, Reverend Brown. He wondered if they would decide to live together. He worried that he would be too far from Minnie and Herman. They had become such a necessary part of his life. He knew his absence would be hard for them too.

When they arrived at the dorm, James lumbered into his new room ahead of his parents. He was 6'2" tall and weighed almost 200 pounds.

"Who are you?" asked the small, dark haired woman standing near a short, skinny boy. The boy looked at James sideways, and then at his mother. She looked James up and down as if he was a member of an alien species.

"I think this is my room, 312," he responded.

"No, that's not possible. This is my Marty's room," she snarled.

"Yes, it's a double. We're both in here," James pressed.

"No, no, no. This won't do. You look too old to be a freshman."

In walked Mark carrying a hammer and screwdriver.

"Oh no!" Marty's mother said authoritatively. "There will be no hammers in this room. I won't allow it!" she bellowed.

"I'm sorry," Mark responded while backing out of the doorway. "I brought these tools so the boys can hang pictures and shelves."

"I'm going to the dean!" the irate woman announced. "Marty, you come with me! We're switching rooms." With that, she stormed out of the room with Marty following sheepishly behind.

James was stunned. He wasn't sure what he'd done to drive away his new roommate.

Mark immediately spoke up. "And good riddance to you!"

"But now I have no roommate," James protested. He walked out of his room feeling like he just lost his best friend, even though he'd never seen Marty before. He wandered down the hallway, glancing into neighboring rooms where he heard the laughter and banter he had been expecting to enjoy. He began thinking that prep school may have been a mistake after all.

With his head hung low, James almost bumped into a boy who looked even more lost than he felt. "Sorry. I guess I wasn't looking where I was going," he mumbled.

"That's okay," the boy responded. He seemed preoccupied, but he finally looked up at the hulking body in front of him. "I can't find my room," he squeaked. "The number listed on my form doesn't seem to exist." He looked at James imploringly.

James perked up. "Come with me!" he said excitedly. "I just lost my roommate. His mother didn't care for my looks. If you like the room, you're in!"

Chan smiled broadly. He was heartened by the welcoming demeanor of this freckle faced giant. "Okay, thanks. I will."

The boys walked side by side to James' room. Each felt rescued by the other. The day had been saved.

Friends and relatives of both boys started trickling in. Soon the tiny dorm room was filled with people, gifts and food. The great babble of introductions could be heard all the way down the dormitory hall. Crammed into the small space was James' family, Reverend Brown and Father O'leary. Mark had his wife Ruth and their three children in tow. On Chan's side were his parents, Hanlee, Uncle Luang and the Rozbruchs. Minnie unveiled the cake and cookies she had carefully double wrapped. Marie cheerfully poured apple cider for everyone. It was a party atmosphere and no one wanted it to end. They didn't want to say goodbye to their boys.

Sulee stood behind the others and took in the scene. She was most curious about the mother of her son's new roommate. She assumed that this was the fabled American mom to whom so many privileges were awarded. The longer she studied Sonia, however, the more she began to doubt the story she had cobbled together in her mind. Before her was a very young woman who appeared somewhat distant and restrained. She was dressed plainly and her hair seemed to be arranged to hide her pretty features. Sulee was fascinated by Sonia's timidity and her childlike adherence to her mother's body. At times she noticed the woman grasping Marie's sleeve as if afraid to let her move too far away. Sulee began to sense that this family had also been traumatized. She felt a growing empathy for them as the day progressed.

Father O'leary made a toast. "To James and his new roommate, Chan. Here's to two remarkable young men who have already proven themselves admirably capable of handling life's twists and turns. May you have a great year!"

Uncle Luang spoke next. "I have no doubt that Chan will live up to the challenges before him, in school and beyond, as he has always done. After all, he comes from a long line of leaders on his father's side. The strength of Genghis Khan, the noble Mongol warrior, is in his blood and it has helped him survive and thrive to this glorious day of new beginnings. It was Chan's good fortune to meet another like him." He lifted his glass. "Good luck to James and Chan!"

Marie was stunned when she heard what Luang had just said. The name 'Genghis Khan' was very familiar to her. Her late husband and his family proudly traced their roots to him. She remembered when, at holiday dinners, the talk always turned to their brave ancestor. She looked around the room, caught Luang's eye, cleared her throat and decided to add what she knew. "I'd like to give my best wishes to the boys who are actually more alike than you may know. Uncle Luang spoke of Chan's relation to Genghis Khan. The first James Gengia, my late husband, James' grandfather and namesake, was also a descendant of the great warrior Khan! How's that for a coincidence? These two may be distant cousins!"

At first, there was silence in the room as the group tried to figure out in what way the boys may be related. They all started to voice the various possibilities. They grew louder and more excited until James held up his hand for quiet. "Whether we are cousins or not, I felt a kinship with Chan the moment I met him. We will look after each other and help each other from here on out."

There was a loud "here, here!" in the room.

James had quelled the chatter in the room with his appeasing statement but deep in his heart he was far from unmoved by the revelation that another new relative may have just dropped into his life as if from an over abundant sky. Though he was generally warm and welcoming, it was unnerving to have to keep adjusting to his ever changing sense of self. Grandma Marie had never mentioned his grandfather's roots before. He had no knowledge of his relation to some old warrior named Genghis Khan. He wondered what else he didn't know. He did not like the feeling of uncertainty he was experiencing and this led him to once again decide to make some changes in his life.

James realized that his naive manner of looking at the world left him exposed to the sorts of shocks and surprises which, whether good or bad, upset and rattled the very ground under his feet. The way he saw it he had two choices. He could enclose his vulnerable self in a hard shell of protection to repel any further disturbances, or he could strengthen himself and face the unpredictable world with the assurance of his ability to prevail. He chose the latter and, in the end, he had to admit to himself that knowing he had warrior blood made that choice easier. He decided he needed to know more about this Genghis Khan character.

His roommate noticed that James was thrown a bit off balance, but he didn't understand this reaction. Throughout his life, Chan had been carefully schooled in his ancestry by his uncle and his parents. The Chinese venerated their origins and generally assumed they descended from great and noble people. They credited long since dead ancestors with the traditions and customs that gave their lives meaning and purpose. Their heritage made them feel steady and strong in an otherwise chaotic world. They worshipped ancient gods and assumed that as long as they were faithful to their beliefs, they would be safe. Chan was, therefore, more open to new revelations about his connections to the wider world. His strong cultural foundation allowed him to integrate change more easily than James. He reacted with delight to Marie's news. How exciting and surprising life could be! What would he discover next? He couldn't wait to find out.

After everyone said their goodbyes, James looked at Chan and said, "What a send off! It's so quiet now. What do you want to do?"

"Explore!" Chan responded.

The boys left their room and began their four year adventure.

Chapter Twenty-Three

Thus began the boarding school careers of two boys whose early lives could hardly have predicted their current positions. As with most teens, they expected their good luck to be unlimited, but they were both smart enough to realize that they had to take full advantage of the options before them. They immediately began to operate as a team. Each somehow made up for what the other lacked. Chan, rarely a deep thinker, tended to rush ahead into new experiences and ideas, often with little caution or forethought. James, on the other hand, methodically planned every step. He served as the lookout. He made sure they were always safe. It was also the case that neither boy was left to fend for themselves. The families on both sides hovered close by.

James attempted to buckle down and concentrate on his demanding schoolwork. He was distracted, though, by all he had gone through in the previous year. Now that he was away from longtime friends and family, he was free to look back and ruminate on his past. Surely he should feel blessed to have everything he needed and to be afforded so many wonderful advantages. At fourteen, however, he was vulnerable to doubts and worries that were sometimes vague, sometimes specific, but always present. He didn't like thinking of himself as "troubled", but there was no denying his thoughts were not settled. He was often distracted by the facts of his life. Time after time, especially in his bed at night, he replayed the day he met his father. Reliving the hurt he had felt at being kept in the dark by those he trusted was especially painful. James envied his classmates who seemed to have no other cares but their grades and social standing.

Though used to solving his own problems, he decided he needed to turn to someone for help. Instantly, grandpa Herman came to mind. He knew the wise old man would hear him out and work with him to try to unravel the knots in his mind.

During his first visit home, when once again he was in his grandparents' loving house for Sabbath dinner, James asked Herman if he could speak to him privately. The rabbi was not surprised. He took his grandson to his private study where many had sought his advice before.

He knew the boy's life had been turned upside down and he too wanted to sort out issues weighing on his mind. He sat close to his grandson and took his hands.

"I'm so glad to be here with you. We have a lot to talk about, you and I. What comes to mind first is what you're going to call me and your grandmother. It seems to be an unsettled question in your mind."

"Yes, you're right. I'm not sure if you want me to call you 'grandma' and 'grandpa'. It feels funny because I call my other grandmother 'grandma'."

"I see. Well, you could call us 'Grandma Minnie' and 'Grandpa Herman'. That should take care of any confusion."

"Okay. That's a good idea. What about my father and his wife? I called him 'dad' once and he seemed surprised."

"He may have been surprised but I'll bet he was also delighted. He calls me 'dad', so it's already a family tradition. I know it'll take some time to get used to."

"Yes, it will. These are such little things. I really wanted to ask you harder questions."

"You can ask me anything you like. Now that we have some of the basics out of the way, we are free to go anywhere you want."

"I'm not sure if I'm Jewish, Grandpa Herman. I know you, Grandma Minnie and my dad are, but what should I be?"

"Ah, that's a very good question. Our religion has always been very important to our family because it defines how we live our lives. There are rules and laws about everything we do.

You don't know those rules and laws yet. If you decide you'd like to learn more about Judaism, you'll see if it makes sense to you. This is the only way." James nodded in agreement.

"To be Jewish is not just a religious label. It's a way of life. Sometimes it can require a sacrifice to comply. For instance, it isn't always easy to follow the Jewish dietary laws. There are so many foods we can't eat. We have to make sure everything is prepared properly. Some foods can't be mixed with others. It isn't always convenient to stop work and celebrate the Sabbath for a full twenty-four hours. On the other hand, how sweet is the Sabbath dinner? How comforting is it to know that you have a standing date every week for the rest of your life with the people you love?"

"I miss it very much now that I'm away at school." James acknowledged.

"And we miss having you. It is up to you to decide if you want to do what is necessary to carry on the traditions. If you do, you will experience great fulfillment in knowing that you are capable of following through on a commitment with a generous spirit. Considering all this, and much, much more, this is not a decision you have to make right away. It can be dealt with as you grow and mature. Does that help at all?"

"I guess so, but do you have to follow all the rules to be Jewish?"

"That's also a good question, but it's not easy for someone like me to answer because I keep looking for more rules, not less, to follow! That's the way I was raised. Your father could be more helpful than me with this question. He's found his own way, which is different from mine.

He may be the one to guide you as you look for a way to proceed."

As they said their goodbyes, James basked in the feeling that although he would have to wait for life to answer many of his concerns, he now had so many more people who loved him to turn to.

Chapter Twenty-Four

Not surprisingly, Uncle Luang was intrigued by the clergymen he had just met and asked to join them in bible study. They agreed to meet at school so the boys could also attend. Every month the group discussed the upcoming portions of the Jewish and Christian bibles which are read in churches and synagogues around the world. Rabbi Gellerman explained the process to Luang. "Judaism begins with the book of Genesis toward the end of summer, the Jewish new year called Rosh Hashanah. Genesis is the first book of the Old Testament, which we call theTorah or the Five Books of Moses. By the end of the year, all five books, Genesis, Exodus, Leviticus, Numbers and Deuteronomy are read and discussed."

Father O'Leary added, "The Christian bible readings, which often include discussion of the Old Testament, traditionally follow liturgical seasons which include the Advent, Christmas, Lent and Easter. Our group has always taken turns with regard to which biblical readings we choose. Whatever we discuss, I can assure you that no one here is ever at a loss for words!"

Reverend Brown turned to the newest member of the group.

"We are all hoping that you, dear Luang, will expand our horizons and teach us about your religious laws, your beliefs and customs. We're always open to new perspectives."

"Yes." answered Luang. "What I have learned over the years is that the way to add spice to life is to sprinkle it with knowledge from around the globe! I will be glad to share my rich heritage with you, as you have so kindly offered to do with me."

On the surface, this looked like an unlikely clan. The boys, however, refused to be apart. This meant that all holidays, vacations and family activities were planned together, making theirs a truly ecumenical experience. Toward the end of the school year, a celebration dinner was held at Mark's home. Luang brought back books he had borrowed throughout the year from Rabbi Gellerman.

"No, no. Keep the books," the Rabbi protested. "Your keeping the books allows me put into practice what we are about to discuss in this week's Torah portion. It is the idea that society can greatly benefit from occasional forgiveness of debt. It is called 'Jubilee' in the bible and it stems from the Jewish perspective that everything in the universe belongs to the Almighty. We are merely caretakers, therefore ownership is temporary at best. During the biblical 'year of Jubilee', all debts were forgiven."

"So am I to understand the books are a gift?" asked Luang.

"No." Rabbi Gellerman said emphatically. "You borrowed my books and therefore you owed it to me to return them. Because I am instituting my personal practice of 'Jubilee', what you owed is now forgiven."

"But that isn't fair! You owe me nothing that I can forgive," argued Luang.

"It may seem uneven now but we must trust that fairness will ultimately prevail."

"That seems overly optimistic. Your plan cannot always end in fairness."

"It's not my plan! It was written as law dictated by the Almighty.

That is a high enough authority for me! After all, it was the Almighty, to whom we owe our existence, who created 'Jubilee' and commanded we observe it."

"Looking at 'Jubilee' from another perspective," Luang opined, "I propose that it is not dissimilar to the Chinese notion of karma. Cast what is yours out into the world and it will eventually come back to you, perhaps in greater or lesser proportions, perhaps in disguised form."

Chan and James lightened the mood by reminding each other what had been borrowed and not returned over the school year. After much good natured argument, they agreed that James owed Chan a steak dinner and Chan owed a huge dessert in return. Rabbi Gellerman reminded them, "You must both go hungry because those debts are now forgiven!"

As they were about to say their goodbyes and officially end their celebration, James turned to Uncle Luang with a question he had been planning to ask all year. Realizing this was his last chance for the foreseeable future, he pushed himself to broach a subject which had seemed to him too daunting to explore.

"I need to ask you, Uncle Luang, if you could spend a few minutes telling us what you know about the great Genghis Khan. Ever since you and Grandma Marie mentioned the family connection to him I've been curious to hear more."

"Ah, I was wondering when his name would come up again. I'm sure both you and Chan have wondered about this ancestor who looms so large in history but remains such a mysterious figure. The myths about him abound. I have done a fair amount of research into his life and I can tell you that the achievements during his reign are worthy of amazement."

The boys listened intently.

"Ghengis Khan was born almost eight hundred fifty years ago in Mongolia. He was one of several children in a family wrought with poverty and strife. Because of family infighting, Genghis was, at a young age, banished from the household and forced to fend for himself. Imagine a young teen having to make it on his own in a primitive world. Just the basics for survival were probably difficult for even an adult to find." Everyone nodded in agreement as they tried to picture themselves in the same situation.

"Considering this, there is no plausible explanation for the vast accomplishments of the mighty warrior. Ghengis Khan conquered more than twice as much of the earth as any other ruler in recorded history, brutally annihilating all who stood in his way. He subjugated and then united untold numbers of tribes, principalities and small kingdoms to create the countries of Russia, China, Korea and India."

"How can that be?" asked Chan. "How was he able to control such a large area and so many different cultures?"

"I suppose he had local leaders running their communities and paying taxes to him." explained Luang. "Khan's empire was built on a revolutionary system of international law and religious freedom. Trade and the dissemination of knowledge and culture between the many newly connected people was encouraged by the opening of commerce and by the building of more bridges than had ever previously existed."

"Where did he learn to do all that?" James asked in wonder. "Was he self-taught?"

"No one really knows." Luang said in a mysterious tone. "The world-changing innovations and societal transformations Khan created defy the imagination of anyone looking into his impoverished childhood. Yet triumph and thrive he did. One can only speculate on what enabled him and drove him to succeed."

Chan looked at his uncle. "What was it, Uncle?"

Luang shrugged. "I wish I could point to one thing. I wish I had been there with him in his youth to witness his transformation from someone who had been cast out from his family and friends to the man who charismatically led huge armies to victory across two continents."

Mark had a faraway look. "It's as if he was two different people. He had a treacherous side and a benevolent side."

"Don't we all?" mused Luang.

Grandpa Herman protested. "Yes, but we have been granted a choice. We have the free will to decide which side to embrace."

"Perhaps Khan had to learn from his mistakes. He had no one to guide him," Mark speculated. Luang agreed. "It is the lucky man who has sage advisors."

James looked at his father and grandfather. He felt lucky indeed. He let his mind wander to imagine the life Khan was forced to live. The story of Khan's inauspicious origins reminded him of his own deprived childhood. He reminded himself that Chan also had been imperiled at birth. He wondered, *What if Chan and I could achieve great things for the world, spurring each other on along the way?* He looked at Chan, trying to discern if his roommate was having the same thought. He mused out loud, "I'd like to know if he had any close allies or friends encouraging him."

Luang agreed, "Yes, there must have been a few he knew would be loyal. Still, he had to inspire them. Someone has to be the originator. Someone has to dream big."

James interjected, "Maybe Khan was free to dream because he

had nothing to lose. Maybe for him things couldn't get any worse."

"He had nowhere to go but up!" Chan agreed.

"What can the two of you learn from him? " asked Luang. "Assuming he is your ancestor, what is his legacy? If you don't ask yourselves this, what use is it to claim him in your lineage?"

The rabbi chimed in, "Uncle Luang is right. You are both descended from many heroes. If you allow them to inspire you, their lives will have that much more meaning and so will yours."

"For me it means defying fate." Chan said excitedly. "My demise had seemed to be predetermined from the moment of my conception. According to the powers that be in China, my life should have been destroyed. That fact makes me want to fight back and show those misguided tyrants where they went wrong."

"The fact that I'm alive is also against the odds, Chan," said James soberly. "My mother was seventeen and single when I was born. What made her decide to go ahead and allow me to be born? I'm not even sure I want to know! But here I am. I'm going to assume there must be a reason I'm here on earth. Maybe that's what Genghis Khan thought. Why, against the odds, was I allowed to thrive? What is my purpose? There must be a purpose."

"Yes," Grandpa Herman said, "this soul searching and questioning is the legacy left to you by your most courageous ancestors. You are only limited by your own imaginations. I'm looking forward to being a witness to this dynamic duo. I hope it's not too much pressure, but I expect great things. I'm unabashedly encouraging you both to achieve beyond my wildest imaginings. The imperfect, bruised world is yours to heal, young men, the sooner the better."

James felt a chill through his body. He wasn't surprised or afraid. He had always known, somewhere in his being, that his early suffering was in preparation for a life of purpose. Taking a look back at those who had preceded him only confirmed these feelings. He had always been a thinker, a brooder. He had always wondered why he was unable to engage with the mundane concerns of people his age. He had assumed it was a failing he would have to address some day. All at once he realized that he didn't need to fight his instincts.

Chapter Twenty-Five

Sonia and her family had come a long way since that fateful day five years earlier. Mark understood his obligation, not only to James, but also to his son's mother. His father spurred him on to help Sonia get started in a career which had been impossible while she was raising their son. Though unmentioned, Mark's phone calls to James and his immediate recognition of his son exposed the fact that he had known all along that Sonia was carrying his child while they were still in high school. He had been so afraid of the repercussions that he said nothing to anyone about it. He had secretly followed Sonia and, when he realized that she had given birth, he felt an overwhelming desire to see the child. He didn't dare approach Sonia openly. He watched her from afar as she walked the baby around town. How he ached to take a peek at the baby in the carriage! As the years passed, he agonized over ways to make contact with his child. He finally decided to call the Gengia household on the chance that the boy would answer the phone. After several attempts, Mark finally heard his son's voice. He was overcome with joy. He wished with all his heart that he could be part of James' life and help him as he grew but he was paralyzed by fear and shame.

The guilt Mark lived with for years was greatly alleviated by seeing to it that James and his mother had a chance to fulfill unmet dreams. He and Ruth made sure that mother and son were included in all holiday and birthday celebrations. They wanted the children to get to know their new brother and to consider him part of the family. Though there was a three year difference in their ages, young Sam was fascinated by his new sibling. He marveled at James' huge body and hoped his own would be similar someday. Playing the role of big brother made it easier for James to find his place in the group. Sam loved it when he helped with school assignments and the twins constantly besieged him with requests for indoor and outdoor games.

Foremost in Mark's mind was following through on his promise to help Sonia find a new home in New York City so she could be near her son. He arranged for her to start working at a local television station, her dream job, as a fill in for weather and traffic announcers. She performed well, with much coaching from Mark's colleagues. They suggested she update her hairstyle and her wardrobe. Sonia agreed. No longer would she cover her delicate features with heavy bangs and long tresses. With a new coif and well applied makeup, the young woman hardly recognized herself. Though she had transformed her look and demeanor, she didn't have to pretend when it came to her mood. Sonia was euphoric. It was almost too good to believe.

Once given the chance to perform, she realized that her early ambition to be on camera was her perfect calling. She came across as unaffected. Her spartan upbringing had served her well.

Chapter Twenty-Six

Prep school social life was almost nonexistent due to the heavy workload and absence of girls on campus. James, especially, missed having female companionship. He very much looked forward to the day when he would be assured never to be lonely again. He daydreamed about having that special someone to care for. He supposed that, in the future, it would be lovely to have a warm and welcoming woman waiting for him at home every night. He modeled this picture on Minnie and Herman. He happily anticipated meeting his Minnie someday.

One day he did. He and Chan were expecting a visit from Sam, James' half brother. He was considering attending their school and he wanted his brother to give him the grand tour and the inside information only a student would know. Sam hadn't mentioned that he was bringing along Lilly, a classmate of his who was becoming more than a friend. The roommates were lying around reading in sweat pants and tees when the visitors arrived. When they saw the pretty girl enter the room with Sam, they sat up at attention and stared as if dumbstruck. James started rearranging his hair and tucking in his shirt in an attempt to look less disheveled. The boys fell over each other trying to offer Lilly a chair. Sam thought this was all very comical. He was surprised that the presence of an attractive female could cause such a commotion.

After the duo had seen the school and left, James breathed a deep sigh and announced, "That girl does not look fourteen!"

Chan agreed. "She's a knockout!"

"Oh no, I saw her first!" James retorted.

The boys raised their fists. "Dukes up!" challenged James. They began sparring. Finally, Chan gave his friend a left hook to the shoulder and said, "Too tall. I want my woman looking up at me. I want to be lord and master."

"Oh, the great Ghengis Khan surfaces! I was wondering when that would happen."

"Well," retorted Chan, "if you steal that girl from Sam, who actually saw her first, then I guess we could say you came by your treacherous ways honestly, courtesy of King David!"

"Touche! I knew Grandpa Herman was making a mistake in over educating you."

"Back to the subject of the girl, my friend."

"No, I don't want to talk about her until I find out how my brother feels about her."

But James couldn't get Lilly out of his mind. He tried to remember all the details of her face.

He knew her eyes were blue and she had the creamiest auburn hair. She was tall and gracefully thin. It plagued him not being able to remember what she had on. Was she in slacks or a skirt? What kind of shirt was next to her skin? He wracked his brain. He realized he had to see her again.

The love struck teenager went to great lengths to find Lilly's phone number. He called five families with the same last name until he heard a young girl call to her sister, "Lilly, its for you!" When he heard her voice, he became flustered and had trouble explaining who he was and why he was calling.

"Lilly, this is James, Sam's brother. You were here a few days ago to see my school. Do you remember?"

"Oh, yes, of course I do. Hi James. Thanks for the tour."

"I thought I'd call to see how you liked it. Do you think you'd like to come here next year?"

"I liked it very much and I'm planning on sending in my application."

"Oh, I can help you with that! If you'd like we can work on it together."

"That would be so nice, James."

"Are you free this weekend? I can take a bus to the city."

Lilly accepted and the two met at a coffee shop and talked for hours. They had common interests in music, sports and school studies. James felt beguiled sitting across from his new friend. He tried not to stare and appear enamored, but it was no use. As they were getting ready to say their goodbyes, he took her hand and said, "We never got around to working on your school application. Can we meet again?"

"I'd like that. I'll have to tell your brother that I've met with you. He and I have gone out a few times. I don't want his feelings to be hurt."

"I don't want that either. He'll think I'm trying to steal you from him. The problem is, I am."

"Let me talk to him. Maybe we'll be lucky and he won't care."

"I doubt that."

At school the next day, Lilly told Sam that she and James had gotten together. She tried not to depict their meeting as a date but she let him know that she wanted to be free to see other people. Sam's reaction was anger and hurt. He started to walk away and as he looked back at her, he said, "I guess compared to James, I'm younger, shorter and stupider, but, unfortunately for me, I'm not too stupid to know that you are very attracted to my brother."

"I'm the stupid one." demurred Lilly. "I can't even think of a response."

Sam looked at her coldly. "Not necessary." With that he left and did not look back. He decided he would not be attending any future family functions that included James. He had nothing but envy and anger toward his half brother. He was also resentful of his father for bringing James into his life. He knew this whole situation was going to cause friction in his family, but the hurt was too deep to ignore. He couldn't tell anyone how he felt. It was all too humiliating.

James was also hurting. The guilt was strong and unrelenting. Chan was a witness to the drama and he finally spoke up. "You'll have to face Sam eventually so you might as well see him now and open your heart to him. It's the only way to heal both your wounds. He'll have mercy on you. If you believe that you meant no harm, he'll believe it too."

The advice was taken. Rarely did James feel the need to defend his actions, especially to himself. His remorse was extremely uncomfortable and paralyzing. He decided to head for the city to see his brother. He found Sam playing basketball at the playground next to his apartment house. James called out to him and asked if they could talk. Sam walked toward his brother with his head down. They sat on a bench and James offered a sincere apology. But Sam was having none of it.

"Those aren't freckles on your nose, James. That's bull dung! You're no more sorry to have won Lilly than I would be. Why don't you just admit it?"

"Of course I'm happy to have Lilly, but not at the expense of my relationship with you."

"So you want me to pretend that I'm happy for you and that I'm okay with your stealing her from me?"

"No. I don't want either of us to pretend anything. I guess I'm asking you to forgive me."

"Why should I? I'd rather see you suffer."

"It won't just be me that suffers. Our family will suffer if we're not on friendly terms. So will Lilly. I know you're being put in a bad spot and I know I'm the one putting you there. I need you to forgive me anyway. Can you do it?"

"You're turning the whole thing around. If I don't forgive you, I'm the bad guy!"

"You could never be the bad guy. You're my little brother. I need your mercy. I'll beg if you want me to."

"You're being so dramatic! Just forget the whole thing. I don't want you to beg. I can't go on with you this way. Fine. You're forgiven. I'll find a new girl."

"Do you mean it?"

"Yes, yes. Now can we drop this subject? You're giving me a headache!"

"Thank you, Sam. Can I hug you?"

"No!" Sam gave James a hard shove to the shoulder. James

shoved him back, but gently.

Sam smiled sheepishly. The boys hugged before parting.

For the remainder of the school year, James and Lilly saw each other as often as their schedules allowed. Their dates required elaborate planning and perseverance because they lived miles apart and had to rely on public transportation and parents to get them where they wanted to go. James was determined not to let too much time go by between dates. He wanted Lilly to see him as her "boyfriend". He worried that some other boy might try to do exactly what he had done. He was so taken with her, he assumed she would always be in high demand. The new focus on his girlfriend interfered with his school work. He struggled to keep up with his assignments and to keep his mind on his studies. Somehow he managed to keep up his grades and keep Lilly close. As the summer approached, she let him know that she had turned down several offers, most of which would have taken her away for the two month break, so that she would be free to see him. This news put James's mind at ease. He basked in the lovely thought that they were now a couple.

Chapter Twenty-Seven

Chatting with Chan one day before class, James took one of those seemingly trivial steps which alter a man's destiny. At Chan's recommendation, he decided to sit in on a political science seminar, one chaired by the eminent scholar, Dr. Harold Buckley. James knew very little about this topic and he thought he had even less interest in it. It was his senior year in high school and he had decided that in college he would major in the sciences where so many of his questions about life could be answered.

Chan raised his hand toward the end of class. Dr. Buckley called on him.

"I've been wondering about something while you were talking, Dr. Buckley. What do you think would happen to the world economy if a country like China forgave America's debt?"

"Ah, Mr. Khan. Why don't you tell me what you think would happen? You seem to have something in mind. Something good? Surely you wouldn't ask if you thought it would end in disaster."

"No, not at all. Forgiveness could not end badly. That would spoil the notion of karma."

"So you see this as more than a question of economics?"

"Yes! I see it as an act of faith."

"And you think all acts of faith are rewarded?"

"It is axiomatic."

"I'm not sure I understand you."

"An act of faith is a reward in itself. If one is lucky enough to have faith, and also has the courage to act on it, that person is doubly blessed."

"We are now well beyond the scope of this class. I will, however, borrow your question and assign it to the class. Everyone write an essay, whatever length you'd like, answering Mr. Khan's question. In your opinion, what would happen in world markets if China forgave the U.S. it's half trillion dollar debt? This should be interesting, Mr. Khan. We have some of the best young minds in the country in this class. I'll be curious to see what they come up with."

James immediately realized what had given rise to Chan's question. *It was grandfather's discussion of "Jubilee"!* It amazed James that Chan had taken bible study seriously enough to apply the idea to his school work. He realized he was constantly surprised by his roommate's ability to let his mind wander, with little fear, in uncharted waters. James, himself, became intrigued by the question and started to imagine that political science may be more interesting than he had previously thought.

Chan saw this assignment as a challenge. He interviewed all the economic professors at his school about the topic. He ran numbers to determine the dollars and cents costs and benefits.

Finally, at their next bible study, he turned to Rabbi Gellerman for advice. This elevated his paper from excellent to brilliant.

The rabbi did not need to ponder Chan's question for very long. He was extremely well versed in all aspects of the bible and its interpretation. "The first point I'll make about your proposition, which you have acknowledged you borrowed from the ancient practice of debt forgiveness, is that 'Jubilee' is a state of mind. The most important feature of the 'Jubilee' law, as with all Talmudic law, is that it forces human beings to think before they act. They are, first and foremost, faced with the acknowledgement that their most precious possessions do not really belong to them. People are merely temporary custodians of what the Almighty has provided.

Because the law required that every fiftieth year the farming land must lie fallow so as not to deplete it, the community had to come together to plan their agricultural activities in advance, with a crucial eye toward conservation. Respect for the land and the regeneration of the soil became paramount."

Nodding, Chan motioned to Rabbi Gellerman to continue.

"The realization that one could get by with less was relearned in every succeeding generation.

The act of forgiving one's fellow man's debt fostered charitable deeds. In short, the effects of this one law spread from the simple acts of forgiveness and sacrifice into the creation of a more humane and equitable society."

"Thank you, Rabbi. I now have a better understanding of the purpose of the 'Jubilee' law. I had previously seen it only as a solution to a possible debt crisis. But it is so much more beneficial than that. It can serve to restore civilizations! I can't wait to write about this."

Having incorporated all of the rabbi's teachings into his essay, Chan's paper became a commentary on improving relations between nations and generating goodwill between people.

It explicated how economic decisions effect interpersonal and international relationships. His paper was passed around among the professors. One of them, on a lark, submitted it to the financial editor of the largest, most respected business newspaper in the country. Because he didn't know Chan and he didn't expect the paper to be published, the audacious teacher neglected to seek permission from anyone. When word came that the essay was chosen and would be out in the coming weeks, there were mixed reactions in Chan's household.

Excited and proud, Sulee exclaimed, "I can't wait to see our son's name in print in a respected newspaper. What an honor for such a young man!"

Her husband was initially chagrined not to have been consulted about such an important matter.

"The gall of that man to act on his own! If we complained to the administration, it could cost him his job."

"Please don't make trouble for Chan at school." Sulee begged. "He's so happy and he feels so good about his achievement."

"No, I would never do that," Aro said solemnly.

The article was published and Chan was contacted by several news outlets for interviews.

Uncle Luang, fearful of the attention this would bring, advised against any further press coverage. "Your citizenship is registered under the name 'Mi Khan' but you go by the name 'Chan Khan'. Officially, Chan Khan doesn't exist! This may cause dangerous scrutiny. We can't afford to take a chance. We don't know who's watching."

"Uncle, this could very well be my ticket into the top business schools. I must go forward with this great opportunity. If anyone asks I'll explain that Mi is my given name but I prefer to be called Chan after my Uncle Chiang Luang."

"I would never stand in your way. Just remember, your supposed grandmother, Mae Ling, is alive and well in China. She has not heard of the name 'Chan Khan'. Neither has her troublesome sister, Myong!"

When Chan was old enough to be trusted with secrets, Sulee and Aro had sat him down and told him the story of his birth and the family's escape from China. Having never remembered anything but a safe, carefree life in America, he couldn't identify with the fears his relatives tried to instill in him. Chan believed that his uncle's concerns about being found out were ridiculous.

"So you really think they're following my progress in America?" asked Chan mockingly.

"I would not be the slightest bit surprised if they were." answered Uncle Luang in a most ominous tone. Chan realized that had he asked his family about submitting the essay, the answer would have been no, with Uncle Luang casting the deciding vote.

Chapter Twenty-Eight

The people left behind in China were, in fact, very curious to know how their "family" was faring in America. Travel outside China was becoming more common. Members of the older generation were not apt to venture overseas. Younger people, especially students, however, were eager to go abroad. One of Mae Ling's grandchildren, Dao Ming, made plans to attend college in the United States. At the age of eighteen, having completed her studies preparing her for university, she applied for a student visa and was granted admission to a New York university. She was eager to see the world and to meet her cousin Mi. She thought they'd have much in common as he too was now at university. She hoped and expected that he would help her get along in the U.S. Dao wrote to him and informed him of her plans.

When Chan received her letter, he quickly contacted Uncle Luang. Luang was immediately alarmed. He knew he couldn't orchestrate this turn of events. The most he could do was coach Chan on how to conduct himself when meeting Dao Ming. He advised his grand nephew to tread lightly when discussing family, even to feign disinterest! Chan would have to explain why he and his family did not keep in touch with his grandparents and their extended relatives. He should use the excuse that, having defected, they did not want to cause further trouble for the family members left behind.

The day of their meeting came and Chan readied himself by remembering that Dao Ming believed her father's sister, Xin, was alive and well! She had no knowledge of the fact that Sulee had assumed Xin's identity after her death. Chan wondered how he would maintain this charade. He began to feel pangs of guilt for the deception he was about to perpetrate. He knew he had no other choice.

Chan sat in the lobby of a run-down midtown hotel waiting for his "cousin" to appear. After what seemed like an eternity, a tiny Chinese teenager bounced in smiling. He noticed immediately that she was a beautiful girl with long, jet black hair and delicate features. She favored her lovely grandmother in looks and demeanor. He greeted her quickly, afraid to look in her eyes lest she figure out the ruse. Dao Ming was bewildered and disappointed by his attitude. She tried as hard as she could to engage him, but to no avail.

They spent the day together as Chan had promised, touring the city and exploring the campus of Dao's new school. They exchanged furtive glances but spoke very little, even though Dao's English was excellent. She assumed her cousin was only spending time with her out of obligation and she began to feel an overwhelming loneliness as the day progressed. If this was how family treated her, how would strangers react? When she and Chan began to say their farewells, he could see tears in her eyes.

"Are you going to be alright on your own, Dao?" He asked, finally showing interest in her.

"I'm very grateful for the time you've given me. It's just that I feel so alone here. I was hoping to meet with the rest of the family. Would that be possible? Grandmother seemed to think I would be invited to your parents' home. She made me promise to send pictures of you and your mother. It's been a long time and she so misses her daughter and grandson! Do you think that could be arranged," she asked again pleadingly, "or will this be our last and only meeting?"

Caught off guard, Chan fumbled for words. "I guess I could ask my mother. I'll have to call her.

She hasn't been feeling well lately. Uncle Luang is old too. They live pretty far away. Of course they'd love to meet you. I'll let you know." He gave her a hug and left her standing in front of her new dorm alone. He looked back and felt sorrow for the sad figure he saw. He called his mother as soon as he could.

The Khan family was faced with a new problem. Dao Ming, the granddaughter of Mae Ling, wanted to visit her supposed family and take pictures to send home! Uncle Luang once again strategized.

"We have to let her come or there will be suspicion. Chan has already told her that you are not well, Sulee. We'll say that you have migraines and must wear a hat and glasses to shield your eyes from light. Chan can also wear sunglasses and a bandanna, as many his age do now.

Hopefully, with these disguises, you'll pass as Xin and Mi."

Everyone agreed and Dao Ming was invited to come by train the very next weekend.

Chapter Twenty-Nine

The family reunion, though awkward at first, went well. Dao Ming felt welcome. She brought pictures of her parents and grandparents and her genuine interest in all things family endeared her to the Khans. The plan to disguise Sulee and Chan, however, failed. As soon as Mae Ling saw the photos that Dao sent home, she knew that the woman passing herself off as Xin was an imposter. A mother knows the contours of her daughter's face and the shape of her body. She wasn't sure who the woman in the picture was, but she was sure it was not her daughter. Mae Ling also knew, beyond a doubt, that the young man was not her grandson, Mi. It was the shape of his eyes that gave him away. Even under the sunglasses she recognized the round eyes of Aro, who she remembered well. Though she was confused and upset, she said nothing. She was now a widow and the only person in China who could confirm her beliefs was her sister, Myong. She didn't dare confide in Myong lest the angry woman cause trouble for everyone. Mae Ling decided to write to Luang and ask for an explanation. She felt confident that their past warm feelings would ensure his honest reply.

Myong demanded to see the photos sent by Dao. She knew immediately who she was looking at and she was outraged. All her previous suspicions were confirmed. She also said nothing but her vindictive mind went to work on a way to punish them all. She was singularly focused on seeing to it that they were exposed.

The day of the visit had another outcome that Chan could not have predicted. Dao stayed glued to his side at all times. Her guileless charm softened the hard stance he had intended to maintain with her. She curled up next to him on the sofa like a kitten and he responded by petting her reassuringly. Her warmth was intoxicating. Chan was in a quandary. He knew this was not his cousin. She was, in fact, no relation to him at all. He also knew that she believed she was innocently showing love to her long lost relative. The love he was beginning to feel was not innocent, however, and he was unsure how to proceed. Of course this did not escape the watchful eyes of Uncle Luang. After the visit, he and Chan had a long talk during which Luang made it clear that his nephew should discourage Dao from trying to become a close friend.

The warning was no use. Chan saw quite a lot of Dao Ming during their years in college. He told himself that this was not of his design. His "cousin" unabashedly insinuated herself in his life. She phoned every day and often showed up at his dorm unannounced. She was lonely and she had so many questions and only Chan had the answers. He tried not to encourage her, as per the advice of his uncle. The truth was, he didn't try very hard. His objections to her intrusions were not made clear. He had to admit to himself that he looked forward to her calls and visits. She was beautiful, intelligent and fun. He found her so warm and welcoming. She held his hand and felt no shame in nestling into his strong body.

The two young students knew their relationship was special. They had family and cultural history in common, yet they each had unique experiences the details of which the other wanted to know. Dao began to open Chan's eyes to the truth about life in China. Before meeting her, he had felt little interest in his country of origin. He proudly thought of himself as an American and though he loved the quaint Chinese traditions and ideals expressed by his family, he did not identify with the country of his birth. He considered the China of the present a mystery he had little desire to solve. Here before him was the key to the puzzle that was his homeland. All he had to do was ask and Dao willingly and knowingly answered. He began by asking her what she missed most.

"What makes you homesick these days? Is it your family, your friends, or being in China itself?"

"Definitely my family. That's one of the reasons I love to be with you! My friends at home were fine people, but, everyone is so fearful of speaking their mind. No one can be truly close and honest without taking a huge risk."

"What kind of risk? What do you mean?"

She had a distant look in her eyes. "Something happens to the morale and the ethos of a people when they are under such strict control. Their minds are as constricted as though they are in a vise. They become wary and experience paranoia, even toward their own families.

Indeed, they are encouraged and rewarded by the government to turn in anyone suspected of harboring negative thoughts about the communist party."

"Did anyone you know ever do that? Or is this just something you suspect could happen?"

"Unfortunately, this is a reality that I have seen among my friends and neighbors. Every aspect of our lives is seen as a testament to our loyalty to the government and the party. That is why the world is now seeing people act so greedy and unethically in business. It is the one area where we can express ourselves. It is like a vent in a highly pressurized vat has been opened.

The steam isn't just escaping, it's bursting out. The people are unable to control their lust for this limited amount of freedom. Because our rights are granted at the whim of the few officials at the top, everyone knows they can be taken away at any time." She looked at him and smiled wryly. "China does not recognize the inalienable rights of all men as endowed by their creator!"

Chapter Thirty

Chan's concern for the country of his birth was gradual at first, but as he began taking an unfiltered look at the reality in China, he became increasingly bothered. He had vivid dreams in which he saw grotesque suffering. He awoke many nights with a start and spent hours unable to sleep, imagining all the ways he wanted to help. He researched the vast systems and unwieldy web of ropes which bound China in thought and action. He grew frustrated and he took it out on his uncle.

"How did you justify, in your mind, turning your back on your country and your people all those years ago?" he asked Uncle Luang.

"We had no choice! If you'll recall, and of course you were too young to remember, you and your mother were stuck underground, hiding from, not only the authorities, but from the whole village! There was no record of your birth. We perpetrated a fraud! Escape from China was the only answer and luckily our chance came in time. Going back would have meant prison for us all, but maybe not for you because you were so young. I do love my country and my people.

I dearly miss my work, my calling as their doctor. Do you dare judge your parents for saving your life?"

"No, no. The whole story is so sad and so inexplicable to me. I'll never understand a system like that. What kind of government treats people the way they do?"

"Again you judge too harshly. I'm not in favor of totalitarian regimes but I can't imagine the equitable solution to famine due to overpopulation. Is the government's duty to its current citizens or to the unborn who threaten the existence of those citizens? As a doctor, I've struggled with triage decisions. Coming to terms with one did not make the next one easier.

Until you're in charge, you can't know what it is to make life or death decisions for other people.

Harsh becomes practical. Practical becomes normal. Everyone but the most rebellious conform."

"Are you saying that you and my parents were the most rebellious?"

"Yes."

"I think the most rebellious try to change the system, not run away from it."

"Then, my brave nephew, go back and get to work!"

"I will!" exclaimed Chan. "I will do that some day. You will see."

Luang thought it wise not to tell his nephew that it was also his dream to return to his homeland some day. Though he was secretly proud of Chan's distress about the fate of the Chinese people, he didn't want to inject his opinion or influence his nephew in any way. He believed a life changing decision was necessarily personal. Still, he silently advocated for Chan to return to China. Luang prayed for the day he could see his country again. He longed to be among his people. He had a strong desire to fulfill the dream of a relationship with the only woman he had ever wanted, his lovely Mae Ling. He had provided a complete reckoning of the harrowing events that led to the false identities seen by her in the family photos. Although her heart was broken by the revelation that her daughter and grandson had died, she forgave Luang for the deception. She knew he and his family had acted to do the least harm in their quest for survival. The previously thwarted lovers began a secret correspondence. They both hoped that they might one day be together and live out their remaining years enjoying the love they both longed to express.

But how to accomplish this final miracle eluded Luang. At age sixty-eight, though hale and healthy, his appetite for risky exploits was greatly diminished. He could hardly fathom how he had dared to accomplish what he had in the past. Chan's new interest in his mother country made the once fearless doctor realize that he was giving up on his dreams without even a fight.

He had a hard time reconciling the feeling of defeat with his former glory.

Later that night, when he slept, Dr. Luang dreamt he was holding a baby. The baby smiled at first but soon it seemed to be struggling for air. He shook the baby and held it upside down to clear its lungs. Every time he checked to see if it was breathing, the baby's face changed. First it resembled his sister, Ling Chi, then his nurse, Xin, then her son, Mi, and finally, Chan. Just before waking, as baby Chan began breathing again, the face turned into that of the young man he had saved so many years previously. He saw the face but couldn't remember the name. All of a sudden he saw the young man's father standing beside him and the name came to him in an instant. He woke with the name on his lips.

He cried out, "That's comrade Lu! The way forward was there all along!" Luang's mind went to work. *I will write to him. I will remind him that, for saving his son's life, he promised to be of help if ever needed. I will tell him about the advancements I have made with my herbs which rightfully should be benefitting the*

Chinese people. This may inspire him to help bring me home. Party leaders are nothing if not practical. In any case, I have nothing to lose.

The plan was now gloriously afoot. The next day, Luang felt as if every step he took bounced him ten feet high.

Chapter Thirty-One

In the years since his fateful encounter with Dr. Luang, Comrade Lu had become an under secretary to the President of China. He had seen to it that his son also climbed the ranks of the communist party. But Yu was a reluctant politician. He was only in the government to please his father. From an early age he had shown himself to be a talented artist and this was where his real ambition lay. There was no bucking his father's authority. He put his dreams on hold. When he received Luang's letter, Secretary Lu didn't have to jog his memory. How could he forget the man who saved his most beloved son? He recalled how disappointed everyone had been when they learned that the brilliant doctor had abandoned his country.

Luang was now asking for his help and a promise was a promise. He knew this would be no easy task and that it would require time and planning. Lu thought deeply about the best way to proceed. His letter in response was encouraging, but it also urged patience. He wrote, "Years ago I watched as you skillfully worked to bring my son back from the brink of death. I will now use my skill and determination to bring you back from your long absence. It was not easy for me, back then, to stand by and entrust Yu's life to you. Now I must ask you to do the same. What you have requested from me will require tactical planning and may take several years, but I firmly believe it can be achieved. Please do not try to contact me again nor take any other steps toward your goal. Until we meet again, Lu."

Chapter Thirty-Two

After a very successful four years of college, Chan gained admittance to the graduate school of his choice. His only regret was that James would be thousands of miles away at a school in New York. They had been together for eight years and the bond between them had grown strong. For all purposes, they considered themselves brothers. Now they would go their separate ways. Chan felt that in order to grow and mature to their fullest potential, it was necessary for each of them to branch out into the world. He knew they would still remain close. He believed they would both benefit by making it on their own for a time.

James was less sure the separation was for the best. He had become accustomed to sharing his every thought with Chan - to whom he could tell anything. He was totally nonjudgmental.

He helped James sort out life's many dilemmas and for that, and for the emotional tie they had, James cherished his longtime companion. He feared there would be no one to fill the void.

Even Lilly, his true love, wasn't always able to handle the questions and concerns James posed. Often he kept his thoughts to himself because he didn't want to burden her with notions he could so easily toss around with Chan. He questioned Chan's decision. "How can you leave just like that? What about your family? What about me?" Chan looked right at him and explained how he felt. "I love you. You are my brother. I also love my family and I'm grateful beyond words for everything they've done for me. But I need to begin facing challenges on my own. I'm afraid that if that doesn't happen I will not become the complete person I wish to be.

It's not that I want danger to come my way, but I need to feel I can face it alone if it does."

James nodded as he spoke. "As you're speaking I realize I don't have the same concerns as you. I don't feel the need to make it on my own because from a very early age I often felt very much alone. My mother and grandmother were there, but they were always worried and distracted. I didn't want to burden them with my needs, so if I couldn't solve my own problems, they went unsolved. It seemed like I was always facing crises and not not knowing which way to turn. I learned by trial and error. It wasn't until my early teens, when I met the other half of my family, that a huge burden was lifted. I never want to have to go it alone again. You were lucky, my friend. But if you want to fly away from the nest, then that is what you must do. You will be sorely missed."

The two friends parted ways for the ensuing four years, always keeping in touch by phone and letter. In some ways it was easier to express emerging ideas and theories to each other while they were apart. James realized he was now freer to think about Chan and to reminisce about their time together and the many ways they had helped each other. Instead of making plans together, he could now consolidate his memories into a coherent narrative and make sense of what had been a unique relationship. He loved to discuss Chan with Lilly. She was always intrigued by his stories of their early lives and the way they found each other and healed wounds from their pasts. She had never known two men who had such strong mutual feelings; she felt the need to question James about the nature of his emotions.

"James, have you ever thought you may be bisexual?"

He did not look surprised by the question. "I will admit that several people have asked me that. I've never asked myself that, however, because it never crossed my mind. Don't get me wrong. Chan does turn me on, but in an intellectual and spiritual way. He unleashes my creative side which is usually hiding in the background of my mind. No subject, no dream, regardless how improbable, is taboo for him. He's as close to a free spirit as I've ever met. My brain treasures his brain. Maybe that means I am a lover of a man, but you are the one who turns on my body. Does that make any sense?"

"Yes, and I'm glad you're able to love another man in the way you describe. It explains your nurturing spirit. The heart has many rooms. It's good to fill them with as many cherished people as possible."

"Very early on I felt protective of my mother and grandmother. Chan has expanded my horizons. He has visions of protecting and nurturing all the people in the world. He has a knack for taking the best of what he has learned and turning it into endless plans for bettering the lot of mankind. I'm right there with him. We bounce ideas off each other and the results are often startling. If we had the power to change it, the world would be a much better place."

Lilly looked at her boyfriend and saw the amazing man he was becoming. She wanted to be part of his future. She had no doubt that his dreams would come to fruition someday.

Chapter Thirty-Three

Dao followed Chan to a school in California and their relationship intensified away from the prying eyes of family. One day, as they sat dreamily under a tree, pretending to study, Dao looked up at Chan with eyes of yearning.

"Is it ever permissible to marry one's cousin?"

He looked back at her and decided the charade had gone on long enough. "Our love has grown beyond what one has for a relative. You are my true love and I do want you for my wife. I've known this for quite some time. You are the woman I adore and trust above all others. I am so happy to tell you that this is perfectly permissible because we are not cousins. Other than planning to be husband and wife, we are no relation at all!"

As Dao's expression went from disbelief to elation, Chan told his beloved the story of his birth and all it had entailed. He begged her forgiveness for keeping such momentous secrets from her. She cradled his head in her hands and smiled. "My only regret is that you and your people suffered in pain and fear. The joy you have given me by loving me and confiding in me is beyond words. There is, however, still a problem. I can't tell my relatives in China everything you have just told me. Aunt Myong will use the information against you and your family. You will never be able to return to your homeland, even for a visit. She would have no second thoughts about turning you over to the authorities. The true story of your past must remain untold. That means the rest of my family will never condone our union. They will all think I am marrying a first cousin!"

153

Chan acknowledged the dilemma. "I've thought about it and I have decided to ask my uncle if your grandmother, Mae Ling, may at least be told the truth. They have been very close and have remained in secret contact."

Dao looked at him with knowing eyes. "I'm not as surprised to hear that as you may think. My mother told me long ago that Grandmother always held Dr. Luang in deep affection. This is a good lesson for us, my darling. There are no secrets! There are only difficult and often painful truths inevitably making their way out of hiding." Chan looked at her sweet, sincere expression and was reassured that he had found a rare girl, wise beyond her years and beautiful beyond her appearance.

Chapter Thirty-Four

With Chan unavailable for their usual exchange of ideas, James took a chance and posed a question to Lilly, the only other person he could trust with his fanciful musings. "Lilly, I have so many ideas for this country. Do you think I should set my sights on being president some day?"

She took a step back and looked at him with a stunned expression. "You're kidding, aren't you?"

"No, I'm serious," he replied.

"This doesn't happen because you will it! You have to be chosen for reasons neither of us could possibly fathom."

"That may be true, Lilly, but the pool of candidates most likely includes those who have expressed interest in the job, don't you agree? For years I've dreamt day and night of all the changes I would make in so many areas of concern in our country."

"Which is it, day or night?"

"Why would it matter?" he asked, perplexed.

"It matters because your daydreams are about what you want to do to the world. The dreams you have while asleep are about what you think the world wants to do to you."

"Yes, I guess you're right. I daydream about elaborate plans, sometimes down to the smallest detail. When I sleep I often find myself in situations which seem to exist independent of my doing. Curiously, I always prevail."

"I don't find it curious. You have so much faith in yourself and your ability. You amaze me, James. I never know what's coming next."

"I hope that's a good thing."

"It's a very good thing. In fact it's a wonderful thing!"

Lilly looked lovingly at the young man before her. She was amazed at how lucky she'd been to find someone who so fully shared her values and goals. She was a serious student and she often pictured her future including a life of family, learning and fulfillment in a career. She realized that James had all the qualities she could ever hope to find in a husband and father.

He was kind and nurturing. He was tall and adorably handsome. He was as smart as a whip, but more than that, he had a curious, searching quality that she believed would lead to great wisdom some day. She knew she wanted to grow old and wise with him.

Chapter Thirty-Five

At the close of their post graduate educations during which Chan acquired a law degree and James gained an MBA, both young men secured jobs in New York City. These were happy years for James. He was in love with Lilly and he wanted to ask her to marry him. His mother was steadily progressing with her career. After a long, intense courtship, Grandma Marie had married Reverend Brown and was happily living in his home in upstate New York, near their oldest and dearest friends, Father O'leary and the Gellermans. Although they were in the twilight of their years, their romance was strong and fulfilling. James and Chan lived and worked in close proximity and spent many after work hours talking and socializing together.

Just when James thought his life was exactly as he would have planned it, Chan dropped a bomb. He confided that his family was seriously considering returning to China for good. There were so many reasons for each of them to want to go back. His grandfather, Anlee, was gravely ill and Sulee wished to be with him at the end. Uncle Luang longed to spend the remainder of his days with Mae Ling. For years, Luang had been corresponding with his never forgotten love, sending caring thoughts and good wishes to let her know she was in his heart.

She returned his feelings with words of love and longing. The two ended each letter with an ancient poem they claimed as their own. *Though far apart, we are still able to share the beauty of the moon together.*

Chan, himself, was miserable without Dao Ming. She had moved back to China after graduate school when her student visa expired. The two young lovers had grown inseparable and now they found the thousands of miles between them intolerable. Chan was also increasingly bothered by what he saw as the poor administration of his native country. He asked himself, *Why has it been subject to so many disasters? Would it be so difficult to put the government's house in order?* He had so many revolutionary ideas and he was itching to bring them back to the nation he now embraced as his own.

The news hit James hard. He had anticipated that Chan would eventually go back to his homeland. He did not think it would happen so soon. Once again he prepared himself for the loss of his closest friend. During their final dinner together, he let Chan know that he might be out of sight, but never out of mind.

"This is not going to be the end of our friendship. The only way I can comfort myself about not having you near is to ask you to promise to work with me in the coming years to put some of our ingenious plans into effect."

Chan smiled. "We are of like mind, my dear James. It is to you I will always look for the strength and support I'm going to need to become what I want to become and do what I want to do in China. Together we'll fulfill our dreams, you stationed on one side of the world and me on the other."

The coming separation from Chan was only a part of James' feeling of sadness and loneliness.

He was also struggling with his ambivalence about his future with Lilly. He told himself he was waiting for the right time to ask her to be his wife. He obsessed about the pros and cons of making their relationship official. James knew that much of his hesitation was due to the lingering guilt he felt about stealing her from his brother. He couldn't bring himself to face the family and especially Sam with the fiancée he wasn't sure he deserved.

One night before Lilly's twenty first birthday James had two dreams. In the first, he was living in an apartment complex waiting with his unruly dog for the newspaper delivery. He knew the paper would be placed out back, on the deck. Instead of walking through the apartment to get it, he chose to go out his front door and walk along the complex with the dog, then double back through all the neighbor's decks. The dog ran ahead, knocking over furniture and generally wreaking havoc. The neighbors were extremely put out, but they said nothing. By the time he reached his own deck, he was so disgusted with what he and the dog had wrought, he tossed the paper aside. He felt ridiculous and ashamed.

In the second dream he was in a field of flowers, each more beautiful than the last. There were stern warning signs throughout the field stating, "Don't pick the flowers!" James obeyed, walking carefully so as not to trample any of the lovely young buds. He came upon one specimen that caught his eye. It stood out because of it's gorgeous color and shape. The flower seemed to call to him, begging to be picked. James could not help himself. He bent down and carefully pulled the stem from the soil. He held it gently and drank in it's aroma. He knew he would keep the bloom forever. When James awoke he took pen and pad and wrote a poem which came to him from a place inside that he never knew existed.

"A birthday doesn't mean a lot unless you've one who cares.

I hope the way I care for you this birthday present bares.

A rose for every year you've lived, for which I thank above,

A ring of gold I add to this, a token of my love.

Twenty red roses all the same, no way to tell apart,

One white rose that's not the same, a feeling in my heart,

That like that one white rose, so rare, so lovely and so new,

A girl so rare, so pretty, so wise, so lovely, Lilly, that's you.

Pray, be my wife and wear the ring which on that rose doth lay,

And with all my heart and all my soul I hope you hear it say,

I love you."

The poem clearly laid out the steps James would take to ask Lilly for her hand in marriage. He wasted no time picking a ring and finding the perfect roses to create the scene he imagined. To his delight, Lilly accepted his proposal. The two young lovers floated home to their families to tell them the news.

Chapter Thirty-Six

The Khan family and Uncle Luang eagerly awaited final permission to re-enter China. This had been arranged, following elaborate negotiations, by Comrade Lu. It had been almost six years since the initial request was made and they had begun to lose hope that Lu had the ability to clear their way. When word came that their return was imminent, their emotions were mixed.

Hanlee decided she would not leave the United States. She had always considered herself an American. She now had a husband and a thriving medical career. She had been carefully groomed by Luang to meticulously carry on his research and practice. Though it remained unspoken, she sensed that her great uncle was relieved to know she would stay behind and continue to tend his extensive herb gardens. Sid Rozbruch was amazed each morning as he surveyed the burgeoning plot of greens from his kitchen window. Over the years, the three doctors had spent much of their free time photographing and cataloguing the herbs born of the treasured seeds smuggled into the country by Luang. Their work helped to advance the increasingly popular field of alternative medicine. Hanlee saw it as her calling to carry on the efforts begun by Luang. Her specialized knowledge was invaluable to the medical community in the United States as it incorporated ancient Eastern remedies into their treatment plans. Sulee and Aro dreaded the day they would say goodbye to their daughter. They were also sad to part from their cherished friends, Sid and Helen Rozbruch and all the other neighbors and coworkers to whom they'd grown close. Despite these regrets, the family once again uprooted themselves and made their way back to their homeland.

At first landing, the re-immigrating group felt a strange sense of disorientation. They had few people to socialize with. Everything seemed foreign and unwelcoming. For Chan and Luang these feelings were alleviated because they knew they would be reunited with the women they loved. The Khans moved in with Sulee's father, the ailing Anlee. He had hung onto life knowing that his loving daughter would be with him at the end. When he finally beheld her after such a long separation, he let go of his struggle and breathed his last breath while she sobbed and cradled his weak bones in her arms.

Sulee and Aro soon realized they could not remain long in their old village because there was great risk that old friends and acquaintances would begin to think back and figure out Sulee's real identity. The couple hadn't anticipated the questions they were being asked by the longtime villagers who were trying to make sense of the newly repatriated clan. Sulee struggled to remember to answer to the name "Xin". She was asked repeatedly why she had secretly changed Mi's name to Chan. Their former neighbors grilled Aro about why, after such a notorious defection from their native land, the family did an about face and returned. It was Uncle Luang who first sensed the danger of the situation and convinced them that they could not stay.

"You will have to go back to America. Once again you must sacrifice for the sake of your son.

Once again you must have faith that your selflessness will result in good. Say your goodbyes and leave quickly. Do not worry about Chan. Dao and I will look out for him. His destiny is here. You will watch with pride from afar knowing that his heart and mine are with you."

Chapter Thirty-Seven

The years passed and James prospered. He made his way to top management positions in three large corporations. Prudent investments and frugal habits served him well and resulted in considerable wealth for the Gengias. The family grew as Lilly gave birth, first to a son, Max, and then to a daughter, Debra. The couple forged ahead, both keenly focused on family and career. They were attuned on most issues and this harmony resulted in a happy, serene household.

Success in the business world was gratifying but not wholly fulfilling for someone itching to change the world dramatically for the better. James began discussing the possibility of a career change with Lilly and with his father. Of course, he'd always had Grandpa Herman's ear, but the old man was now very infirm. He still had all his faculties, however, and James longed for his sage advice. On a chilly fall day, he asked his mother and father to join him and Lilly for a long overdue visit to his grandparents and friends upstate. Mark and Sonia jumped at the chance to visit their parents. They decided to include the original bible study group. Everyone was to meet for dinner at the Gellermans.

As they drove through the town where they had spent their childhoods, they saw boarded up businesses and homeless men and women sleeping on sidewalks covered in ragged blankets.

The major roadways were pitted with large ruts. The scene was bleak and dismal. It had the feeling of an abandoned area, certainly neglected and deteriorating rapidly. James was visibly shaken as he commented to his father that he had no idea things had gotten so bad. This was not the town he remembered which, while never prosperous, had always seemed quaint and inviting. They finally reached his grandparents' home and they walked up a pathway that was now more barren and unkempt than it had been even a few months before.

No one answered when they rang at the door, so Mark used his keys. They found Herman and Minnie asleep on the sofa, though it was midday. They gently woke them. Startled and woozy, the couple admitted they had no food in the house to offer for lunch. Mark decided to go to the local kosher market for sandwiches and coffee and before long the family was supping at the table James loved from his youth.

Mark spoke his mind. "You two need some help here. How about you come and live near us?"

"If you're talking about an old age home, we're not interested," answered Herman gloomily.

"I knew you'd say that," retorted Mark. "Do you want to live in my house? We have plenty of room. You know Ruth would love to have you."

"Pardon me for changing the subject. I don't care where I live as long as I live to see my grandson look much less miserable! Maybe we'll move in with him. Grandma has always been able to put a smile on his face."

James acted surprised. "What makes you think I'm miserable? I have a very happy life. I have my beautiful Lilly and our children, all of whom are the lights of my life. Why would you think there's anything wrong?"

His grandmother added her opinion. "It's written all over your face."

As usual, James treasured the way his grandparents read his mind. He admitted that it wasn't only their welfare he was concerned about. "I was truly shocked today when dad and I drove through town. Everything looks so bleak and abandoned. The main road isn't even paved anymore. How did I not know conditions had gotten this bad in my own hometown? I feel like I've neglected a very important part of myself. I cannot express how sad this makes me.

Looking the other way and going on with my life in the city is not going to be an option. What I've seen today will haunt me wherever I go."

Herman stared into the space between them. He couldn't deny that conditions had severely worsened in recent years. "These are hard times for northern New York and for most rural communities across the country. The people have given up. They seem dispirited."

Minnie shook her head in agreement and added, "It feels like a ghost town when I venture out to the market. The gloom is unnerving. Not to mention that everything has become so expensive. Years ago being poor meant living a simple but mostly contented life. Neighbor helped neighbor and the community came together to see that nobody was destitute. Now everyone relies on the government for handouts. The notion of pitching in for the common good has evaporated."

Herman looked puzzled as he went on. "I'm not sure why it happened, but somehow, over the years, our society has come to confuse a loosening of standards and a lack of order with progress. Religious observance has dwindled. Where once people got to know each other through their church, they now live mostly isolated lives with little spirituality to nourish their souls. Young people move away at the earliest opportunity so we are left with a poor, aging population."

James sat up in his chair excitedly. "I think you've given me an idea, grandpa. The only way to bring this area back to life is to lure people here. We'll start with our little town and hopefully it will cause a ripple effect all around us!"

"But James, you don't live here anymore. You have a life and a career hundreds of miles away," Grandpa Herman protested.

James slumped back down in his seat, realizing his grandfather was right. All his ideas and good intentions were pointless because he didn't see how he could effect change from so far away. He began to absorb the hopelessness of the surroundings. He looked around at the faces of his family. In them he saw looks of longing and frustration. The room went quiet as they ate their meager lunch.

Lilly let out a long sigh. "I'm so used to this group having all the answers. I'm truly stunned to see you all give up so easily. Often, when a task seems daunting, breaking it up into small parts is helpful."

"But where to start?" asked James.

Lilly then spoke the words she knew had to come from her alone. "As much as I'm reluctant to admit it, this project will require us to move. If you're serious about taking on the task of rejuvenating this area, we'll have to set up shop here. You, James, will have to reacquaint yourself with the people, the businesses and the current office holders. I will have to put my career on hold and our children's lives will be disrupted. This is a commitment I'm not sure I'm willing to make."

James looked astonished. "I'm so glad it is you who is suggesting this because I would not have had the nerve to ask you to abruptly change your life and move here. All I ask is that you think it over before deciding. In fact we'll all need to think this over."

"If we think too much we'll get bogged down again like we were a few minutes ago. All that's required to start a project of goodwill is the goodwill. We've got that," said Herman authoritatively.

"You're right, Herman," injected Minnie. "When the rest of the group gets here we'll ask them to help us with the details. Are we all agreed?"

A resounding "Yes!" rang out across the table. Lilly knew she was outnumbered and she remained silent.

Later in the day, the others began to arrive. There was much hugging and cheek pinching as they made their way to the fraying but comfortable sofa and chairs. Father O'leary plunked his weary bones into his seat and looked around at his friends.

"I'm so happy to be here! I've been looking forward to this all day. We're together again. Everyone except Chan and Luang. Maybe we'll call them later and tell them how much they're missed."

"Great idea Timothy," agreed the rabbi. "We may have important news for them. We have much to discuss today. I'll let James tell you his plans. We need input from everyone." Reverend Brown looked eagerly at James. "Don't keep us in suspense! What's going on?"

They were filled in on what had been discussed earlier. There were many nods of understanding and agreement as James began to express his concerns about conditions in their town. The prevailing reaction in the room was excitement and hope for the future. The optimism they started to feel was based on their faith in the capable young man they saw before them. This was the James they adored coming into his own and becoming what they all had hoped he would eventually be. This was the fruit of all their careful teaching and grooming. There was no small talk in the old group that day. They got right down to mapping out their boy's political career. The three old men convinced him to embrace the power of the clergy to help him win over a skeptical public. James had no problem accepting their assistance.

Between them, they knew everyone within a one hundred mile radius.

When they finally sat down for a potluck dinner skillfully prepared by the women with whatever leftovers and odds and ends they could find, Mark looked at his father and made an offhand remark that the others took as a prophecy.

"Wouldn't it be funny if our meeting today led to the future president of the United States?"

"Who better than James to trust with the country's future?" blurted an excited Sonia. There was an enthusiastic nod of agreement by everyone in the room. She beamed at her son who showed no sign of surprise.

"It's thanks to all of you that I have the confidence to hear those words and consider them a possibility. I could not contemplate taking on this new venture if I didn't have your support. I know how lucky I am to have a loving team on my side."

"You always will," replied Grandpa Herman.

James looked at the faces before him and tears came to his eyes. He understood that these people were his lifeline. He remembered back through the years how each had nurtured him and helped him blossom into the man he had become, a man who had come to believe in himself and in his unique strengths. He considered himself blessed. Though he knew they didn't need to be told of his gratitude, he couldn't help but express what he so deeply felt. Now that they were all willing to dare to see James' future as unlimited, he felt as if he had been lifted to a new vantage point from which he could see beyond doubts and fears and toward the realization of his loftiest dreams.

In the back of his mind, James had often flirted with the idea that someday he would run for president. He had total faith in his ability to make rational choices and to block out the noise that often muddles decisions. He prided himself on his fairness and balanced political views.

He now realized that those who knew him best trusted him beyond the bounds of friendship and family. It occurred to him for the first time that it was up to him to embrace the power he now knew he held and to apply all his efforts to using it for his most ambitious plans.

In the ensuing weeks James embraced the strong pull he felt toward his old hometown. He knew his first task in his new endeavor was to gauge Lilly's resistance to such a radical life change. They discussed, argued and dissected all the repercussions of plan. He made the case that the children were now in high school and were well on their way to being self sufficient. There were several family members with whom they could easily live while he and Lilly were upstate. Lilly responded by pointing out that their serene, almost perfect family life was the result of careful planning and sober judgment. She questioned whether the current plan would cause an upheaval to all they had created. All of her arguments were presented in a halfhearted manner because she innately understood that if she wanted to keep the optimistic man she had married, her husband's vision could not be denied. After the initial shock and reluctance to participate in James' life changing plans, she reminded herself that this was exactly why she loved the man. His special gift was that he found hope in the most hopeless situations. He sensed that his town was ready to be led back to productivity and its people to lives of meaning. They had reached the bottom and they were not happy there. This was more than an economic rescue. They had to have their faith renewed. Who better to help them than her ingeniously inspired husband?

After much internal debate, Lilly phoned Minnie and the two women came up with a plan which she shared with James.

"Your grandmother and I have decided it would make sense to swap houses. This will allow us to get started immediately and it will solve the problem of the children's care. They and their great grandparents will look after each other."

James was not surprised. He knew that once his wife was committed to a cause, she would use all her skills to see it to completion. He took her hand and expressed his admiration. "I'm a lucky man," he answered sweetly.

The plan was now afoot. They would move upstate and live in the Gellermans' soon to be empty house. James would enter politics. He would run for local office in the town in which he was raised.

Grandpa Herman was heartened and excited when he heard the news. He and Minnie moved in with the children, telling themselves that they were only doing so to help James put his dreams into action. Debra and Max were delighted with the arrangement. They felt they were being given adult responsibilities. Their grandparents hadn't driven in years, so the teens shared the use of the family station wagon. It was up to them to keep the refrigerator stocked and to see to it that all chores were done. They intended to closely follow the progress of their father's political campaign, cheering him on as only his most ardent fans could do.

Chapter Thirty-Eight

As James and Lilly made the long trek to their new home with their belongings, they began to realize the magnitude of the undertaking they were about to face. Both were lost in thought on the ride upstate, planning the necessary tasks for the days and weeks ahead. Lilly read the to-do list she had started.

"Let's see what we'll tackle first," she began. "Of course we'll have to fill out change of address forms. I'll work on updating our licenses and getting new library cards. We'll need to buy new furniture if we're planning on receiving guests. That old sofa will have to be replaced. It's worn to the bone."

"No, no, no!" James brought himself to attention. "Not the sofa. It holds so many memories for me. I was sitting on it when I saw my father for the first time! We can't part with that."

"Can we at least recover the thing?" his wife pleaded.

"Let's just get a slip cover for it," James bargained. "That way I can take it off whenever I feel nostalgic."

"I hope that's not very often, my love," Lilly said chuckling.

"Don't worry. Everything will fall into place. We'll make the house comfortable and cozy like it was when I first saw it. You'll see," he promised.

Having settled this issue, James' thoughts turned to the greater challenges ahead. With no political experience, he would have to improvise and plan a campaign. Although he couldn't bring the whole team of family and friends together again, he intended to kept in touch with everyone daily by phone. His first call was to his grandparents.

Minnie answered and assured him that all was well with the children. "We're settling in and dinner is about to be served. Everyone had a hand in this meal. Grandpa has tasted each dish and given his blessing."

"We wish we were there to share it with you. Give them all our love."

Minnie hesitated. "Before you hang up, I was thinking. You might want to consider enlisting the aid of your brother in your campaign. He's a master of public relations. He's built a career helping business people and politicians polish their images." His grandmother went on to suggest that Sam had the necessary expertise to ensure that James' innovative ideas were rolled out in the best light. Her real motive was that, working together, her grandsons would finally mend their strained relationship. James agreed immediately. He wanted his brother on his side. He knew he would face many dissenters and he needed to have his entire family in his corner.

The first political race James faced was for state assemblyman. He was running against a seasoned politician whose platform was a rehash of tired policies that had failed in the past.

The candidate lacked the drive and imagination displayed by the optimistic newcomer. James and his team put forth their bold ideas for change with vigor. In speeches before a public eager for innovation, he was greeted with cheers and encouragement. He won handily. The people were looking for a break from what seemed like incompetent leadership. A young, energetic candidate with a fresh outlook was long overdue. James took his easy victory as a sign that he could now go full steam ahead and make his dreams a reality. He barely slept after the election because he wanted to correct everything he saw as wrong as quickly as possible.

Deciding to include Sam and his company of media experts to smooth his entry into politics turned out to be a wise decision. Not only did they frame James' lofty ideas in the best possible light before a skeptical public, they also helped him prioritize his goals and properly pace the needed changes. The effect was well-implemented rollouts of new programs and stimulus packages which revitalized the whole area in and around the town. Neighboring municipalities took notice and consulted with their bold colleague. They wanted to replicate his success.

James was more than willing to have his plans spread as widely as possible. He knew that this could only lead to better outcomes for all. He gained wide recognition as the savior of a formerly hopeless situation.

As James forged ahead with one new idea after another, his endeavors were given a huge boost by the election of a new president who admired the optimism and spirit shown by the young congressman from upstate New York. The president had plans of his own for rebuilding the infrastructure around the country and for uplifting blighted areas which had long been neglected. He began consulting with James and incorporating many of his ideas into country-wide revitalization programs, giving credit to the Gengia team whenever it was due.

James gained national recognition as projects were completed and spirits were lifted in formerly down-trodden regions. He received repeated pleas to join the president's administration.

Flattering as these offers were, he held firm to his loyalty to his hometown area. As a result, he gained the trust of the populace. Even the ever-critical media noted that the hero from upstate New York was the kind of political leader everyone longed for and assumed was extinct. There were many who mentioned the name of James Gengia as a very desirable presidential candidate. This came as no surprise to those working alongside the tireless congressman.

James was the type of man people could look up to but not feel intimidated by. His common sense approach led him to ignore political infighting and intrigue. He was not particularly interested in winning friends, nor was he preoccupied with those he opposed. He focused on getting the job done and for this he was rewarded by the voters. He was reelected three times.

Lilly and the children watched as James came alive as never before.

Learning of these developments in his friend's career from afar, Chan was increasingly impressed by James' triumphs. It seemed that every week major newspapers mentioned the young congressman and all gave glowing reviews. This was all the more remarkable because in their weekly phone calls, James never mentioned his success, only his plans to move forward with his many objectives. The two men had always spurred each other to greater achievements. James' victories gave Chan the impetus he needed to press on with his own lofty goals.

Chapter Thirty-Nine

Chan's reentry into China was not without peril. He had at least one determined enemy who was enraged at the family's return. Myong continued to nurse her desire for vengeance against the whole group, especially Luang. Hearing through the grapevine that he was interested in courting her sister, she felt an old wound reopen. At the age of eighty-five, she had little to do with her time other than rehash ancient grievances. When she learned that Chan had governmental aspirations, her spiteful mind began working on ways to bring him down. She thought of very little else. She savored the power her secret knowledge gave her.

Myong had the uncanny knack of knowing when to strike to do the most damage to her perceived enemies. Hearing that the Chinese president was about to retire, she sensed that a major governmental change was coming and that she had to act fast. For weeks the vindictive woman spent all her waking hours talking to herself about her nefarious plan. *I need a contact, someone in the government who won't ask about the source of my information and who won't question my motives. It could be my old comrade, Lu. After all, I was his wife's childhood friend. I was a midwife to her when their son Yu was born.*

As often happens with wicked schemes and the people who spawn them, Myong's instincts were correct. She knew none of the details of Chan's political ambitions but she sensed that an old party regular like Lu would not look kindly on a repatriated upstart. She concocted an elaborate plan to rekindle her relationship with the now powerful Lu family. She speculated that with Lu preoccupied with governmental responsibilities, his wife must be living a lonely, solitary life in her empty house. Myong made several visits to her and quickly ingratiated herself to her old acquaintance. She saw to it that she was invited to the next family dinner during which she intended to corner Lu and inundate him with the incriminating evidence she knew would interest him. She gathered dates, facts and pictures to prove her charges. If asked how she came upon the information, she intended to say that she had always been suspicious of Chan's family, especially the aloof Dr. Luang and his secretive ways. She would explain that, for that reason, she kept a close eye on them all.

The night before the dinner, as she steeled her courage to go ahead with her scheme, Myong fell into a deep sleep with the delicious taste of malevolence swirling around her mind. She began to dream that she was up to her neck in sugary syrup. The color was so bright red, it blinded her. As she wallowed in the morass of sweet goo, she began to have trouble breathing.

She felt her nose and then her mouth become clogged. Her eyes were glued shut. She felt herself sinking. She reached out for help but none came. The sweet revenge was taking her down. She awoke in a pool of cold sweat.

Though she had no clear memory of her dream, when Myong woke up wet with perspiration, she assumed she had a feverish flu and decided to stay in bed all day to recuperate. One day turned into three and then a whole week went by. She weakened from lack of movement and food. She became totally preoccupied with what she thought was a worsening disease, the one which had killed so many of her family and neighbors. All her other thoughts and cares vanished. Myong lived out the rest of her days as a recluse who rarely left her home or even her bed.

Chapter Forty

Days and then weeks had gone by and Luang continued to put off meeting with Mae Ling. He thought of nothing else, but the possibility of an awkward reunion, or worse, a rebuff after so much time apart, paralyzed the man who had no problem being a hero for others. One morning he woke up, looked in the mirror and saw old age staring back at him. He suddenly realized time was running out for him and his beloved. He summoned all his courage and started walking resolutely toward the house of Mae Ling. Looking at the road ahead, he imagined her lovely face. His reverie was suddenly interrupted by a distant figure coming toward him. A strong pull in his stomach tightened into a knot as his eyes reflexively opened wide with dread.

Could it be? He asked himself in horror. *It's definitely a female. I can make out long flowing garments. It couldn't possibly be her. She's a recluse now. She never goes out. Nobody's seen her for weeks. Still, I can't take a chance. I'd better turn around and walk back quickly the way I came.*

As he was about to make his escape, Luang saw the figure wave in a way that was too friendly and warm-hearted to be the foe he imagined. He focused as hard as he could and realized it was his beloved walking, now running toward him. His fear turned to joy as he picked up his pace. Luang and Mae Ling flung themselves together laughing, crying and kissing through their tears.

"I'm home," he cooed in her ear.

"You're finally home," she whispered back.

Chapter Forty-One

A complete outsider to the party elite, Chan worked his way quickly through the ranks by way of his charm and natural talents. Because he had been born in China but had spent his life abroad, he once again had the role of tutor to those around him. His government colleagues turned to him to unlock the riddle that was their adversary, the United States. Chan showed great insight in economic and political strategy. After becoming a party secretary, he positioned himself to be in line for the presidency. Lu's son Yu was also vying for the position. It was the father's dream finally coming to fruition. He was sure his son had the best chance to succeed the president who had been his mentor and strong supporter for three years. Before the upcoming gathering of the Chinese Communist Party's Central Committee, where rivals challenge each other for top leadership positions, Lu spent months coaching his unenthusiastic son on how to project power and show his superiority among the possible candidates.

When his chance came, however, Yu's lack of ardor was all too apparent to the gathered politicians and generals. The meeting went on for three days at the end of which Yu stood up to make a statement. To his father's horror, he gave a heartfelt endorsement to his capable colleague, Chan Khan, to be the next president. Yu turned to his father and explained that his actions were the result of a true belief that Chan was the best choice to pilot the bulky ship that was China.

"The dire economic crises now facing the country threaten to throw it back to third world status.

Our huge manufacturing based economy is stagnating due to the enormous debt of our biggest customer, the United States. Everyone knows it will take an innovative and courageous mind to create a plan to address the ominous prospects for our future. Having lived and worked in both countries, Chan is uniquely qualified to strategize solutions for us. I am convinced of Chan's love of his country and his people because he has returned to both of his own free will with a longing in his heart to enhance our country's greatness. I am also convinced of his ability to govern us because he has shown me the work he has prepared for us to review today."

Yu referred the party members to the voluminous thoughtful reports written by Chan addressing the country's problems, large and small. Upon reading his work, the solutions often seemed obvious. The leaders saw that it was Chan's ability to see China objectively while holding the nation close to his heart that enabled his meticulously planned improvements.

Comrade Lu felt a thick dread spreading deep inside his body while his son spoke of Chan with such praise. He played back in his mind the role he had in the current reality. With all his might he wished to undo his naïve reaction to Luang's letter requesting help with re-entry into China.

He had been warmly touched to think that the great doctor would come to him for help. Lu was so proud that he had achieved enough power and clout to be in a position to pull the necessary strings. He now clearly understood that his desire to appear magnanimous in the repayment of a debt was a blunder born of grandiosity and blind arrogance. What was happening before his eyes on this day was set in motion by his own words and deeds. All the dreams and hopes of a lifetime disintegrated into a smoldering pit in his core.

It was obvious to all that Comrade Lu was stunned and dismayed. Chan stepped up to the fore of the group and spoke. "I thank Comrade Yu for his generous endorsement. I heartily accept the nomination. If this august group of learned leaders selects me to steer our nation, I will do my best to find a course which puts the wind at our backs and the sacred sun in our future.

My proposed plans for China are based on my desire to hear the voices of all our countrymen. We need to know whether or not a system other than autocratic rule cansucceed in our historically suppressed populace. I am aware that several before me haveaspired to bring some form of democracy to China. More than a century ago, the great Sun Yat-Sen attempted this very thing. Perhaps our country was not ready, at the time, for such a radical move. I believe that our fellow countrymen are now far better educated and aware of the political choices before them.

I have devised a program through which each province will select candidates to be voted on electronically and anonymously. Those provincial leaders will then accept a list of items of concern from each city and village. The lists will then be broken down by category and published for all to consider and discuss. Referendum votes will be held. This is to be a first step toward educating the people in the democratic process. Public venues for critiquing the referendum process and its outcome will be made available in every village and city neighborhood. The hope is to foster a spirit of civic participation and cooperation."

Chan was certain that the solutions to China's problems needed to be addressed from the ground up, by the people themselves. While their country could not exist in isolation from the world, heavy reliance on conditions outside it's borders blurred the vision for it's own best interests. For his plan to go forward, he would have to convince his comrades that they were wasting valuable assets and talent by concentrating all their efforts on maintaining their tight grip on every aspect of their people's lives. Loosening that control would free them to focus on the larger issues that begged for their attention. He knew that argument would appeal to their vanity. He also knew the financial crisis they faced made this the perfect time to propose such a monumental change. The gamble was that the leaders would agree to give their people a chance and, just as crucial, that the people would step up and do their part. He truly believed there was nothing to lose. He felt that even an epic failure would be more desirable than the current system and it could ease the way for his ultimate goal of a constitutional democracy.

Comrade Yu was Chan's only ally in his radical scheme. Yu's gentle, artistic nature was perfectly suited to a more liberal view of governmental rule. He agreed with every one of Chan's ideas. He began a campaign to convert his father to their way of thinking, knowing that Lu's voice was powerful within the party. Lu, questioning his own political vision following his dashed hopes, succumbed easily to his son's efforts. This was the support which helped turn the tide of history for the great nation of China. President Chan Khan took office after receiving the unanimous endorsement of the government's central committee.

Chapter Forty-Two

The country lurched forward through debilitating crises during the decades preceding James' presidential run. Frequent natural disasters including hurricanes, forest fires and earthquakes drained the nation's resources. Terrorist attacks and senseless gun violence became commonplace occurrences. Joblessness grew as as technology replaced workers with machines. The continual, unrelenting blows to the spirit of the people was devastating. Many leaders tried, but none succeeded in bringing the legislature together to agree on the monumental changes needed to address environmental, social and economic issues. The political tribalism which split the populace into warring factions resulted from a lack of shared principles and eroding social cohesion. The citizenry longed for a new leader, one whose visions could heal the growing rift between opposing political camps.

When encountering James for the first time in campaign interviews and press conferences, many were intrigued by the notion of a vigorous, dashing young man as their next president. He had a reputation for being energetic and bold, blazing new trails with his direct, problem solving style. Lilly, his most ardent advocate, captivated the people with her modest, resolute loyalty to her husband.

The campaign had a simple message which James put forth in the form of a question:

"What do you want from your government? Should your elected officials continue managing our nation's decline or is now your opportunity to hire someone who has spent his public service career identifying problems and actually solving them? Your vote is your answer."

When asked for the rationale behind the use of a simple inquiry as a strategy for winning the race for the highest position in the land, James responded, "Asking American citizens to step back and consider what they want from their government enables them to put into focus their longings for a simpler time and a sensible leader."

The direct appeal to voters was a rousing success. People who had never taken an interest in political matters began writing long opinion pieces in their local papers about the changes they hoped to see in their local, state and federal governments. They credited the young candidate, James Gengia, with rousing them to participate and vent their frustrations. At rallies across the country the slogan rang out :

"Hear our call! Hear our names! We want action! We want James!"

The result was a landslide victory for the republican from New York.

Chapter Forty-Three

After being briefed by the outgoing president, James realized that the international fiscal crisis was far worse than he had been led to believe. In their daily phone calls, he and Chan lamented the increasingly bad economic news around the world. All first world countries were plunging into a depression.

Three months into his presidency, James had an idea sparked by the eulogy he had just given for his grandfather. Herman Gellerman passed away at the age of eighty-eight. Mark was inconsolable so it fell to James to speak at the rabbi's funeral. He tenderly reminded everyone of Herman's kindness. Though not a man rich in dollars, the wealth of love and knowledge he left behind would benefit his heirs throughout their lives. He told the mourners how the wise rabbi had led a life inspired by the teachings of the Torah which he faithfully passed on to his family and to his congregation. James recounted the lessons his grandfather had taught him, especially forgiveness and charity. His mind wandered back to the day Grandpa Herman taught everyone about the year of "Jubilee". He replayed that lesson to himself throughout the funeral and for the rest of the day and into the night, comforting himself with the pleasant memory.

In his next conversation with Chan, he reminisced about their years of bible study with their learned mentors. "I'll dearly miss having Herman to go to with my dilemmas. I think if he was with us now, he'd point us in the right direction. He'd have a biblical remedy for the world's current crisis."

"I'm sure he would," agreed Chan.

"Do you remember the paper you wrote in high school about China forgiving U.S. debt?"

"How could I forget? You're not suggesting that as a possibility? Yes, I believe you are!"

"All I'm asking you to do is think about it. You saw it as a double blessing back then. Maybe you were right. You were a brilliant student."

"Yes, and now I'm a brilliant politician who would like to avoid making the current world crisis worse!"

"It will only get worse if we do nothing. The projections for the future are not just dim, they're dire. You, and you alone are the spark of light through all the darkness in the world!"

"I need time to think."

"Don't wait too long, my friend. If this is not to be, we'll have to come up with something else soon. We have to act now!

Chan hung up and went directly home to Dao. They agreed to seek the counsel of Uncle Luang.

Briefing his uncle about James' idea and the decision before him, Chan made it clear that he was convinced there were no other steps he and James could take to move their countries, and indeed the world, toward a solution to the crises they faced. He also expressed serious reservations about their plan. He was paralyzed by doubt. Luang reacted with one thought which he spoke aloud. "Sometimes embracing the obvious requires the most courage."

Chan had a puzzled look. He needed more of an explanation than that! He wanted Uncle Luang to either tell him the plan was brilliant or that it was the most foolish idea he had ever heard.

Luang had no intention of satisfying this need.

"You have always had the courage of your convictions. Now you speak as if your instincts are trying to trick you and lead you down the road to disaster. Unfortunately, no one in our long Chinese history has ever traveled this particular road before, so there is no map. You seem to be groping in the dark. But is that really the case? You have said yourself that the idea of debt forgiveness is as old as the oldest religions of mankind. What did those who enacted it have that you do not? It is the bravery of the explorer that creates the path, and ultimately, the map.

I am not schooled in finance nor economics but I see clearly that the person my country has chosen as their most able leader must trust his own judgment and must be willing to act boldly or we are doomed to live in a morass of unsolved problems."

Chan knew that his uncle saw the problem from a different perspective and that he was correct. Other than the scale of the plan, it was not an original idea. It was, in fact, as old as the hills, but it was a radical plan even then. He tried to answer, in his own mind, Luang's question. *What did those ancient leaders have that I am now missing?* The answer was obvious to him now. *Those people took bold steps based on their faith that what they were doing was morally correct and in keeping with their beliefs. From that came clarity and focus. Because they were sure of their goal, finding the most direct path to it was clear.* Chan noted to himself that the ability to focus had not always been his strongest asset. He realized that he had been unsure because he feared his mind was flailing around seeking solutions that were untenable.

The seemingly endless discussions pro and con ended with the two beleaguered leaders deciding to go ahead with the institution of a one time "day of Jubilee" with China forgiving the entire debt owed by the United States. James was deliriously happy at the prospect of saving his country. He knew in his heart that the people were ready to be rescued by any means possible. Their pride was sublimated by the will to come back. They were so unhappy that they were willing to reach out for a helping hand. *Who better to give them that,* James asked himself, *than a country and a people who were longing to regain their humanity?*

Chan, in the end, had few concerns about the coming events. He felt like a child with an exciting secret. He savored the hours leading up to the announcement, playing with the reaction of the world in his mind. He felt he had a free hand in his own country. No one dared criticize a government action after the fact, and since no one knew in advance, he was sure of his position. He expected shocked reactions from the other party leaders, especially the generals, but none would utter a word of disagreement. They would have to support him or face ouster from the government. Chan was more confident than James that the citizens of the United States would hail their president as a hero and a genius for orchestrating the most radical financial coup in history, or at least in the last 3000 years! He was willing to give James most of the credit, even as he planned to explain the benefits of the "Jubilee" to China.

Chan promised him that the disaster would pass by James and his nation and that they would find themselves safe and in a changed universe. "'Jubilee' will be the means of restoring that solid peace and harmony between China and the U.S. so essential to the well being of both."

James smiled to himself as he savored his unwavering affection for Chan, whose virtues he could appreciate since many aspects of Chan's character were echoed in his own. Still, his doubts continued. He remembered the day he and Chan hatched the plan they would now be implementing. As the brazen scheme was now inching closer and closer to reality, he called Chan frantically one night. "What are we doing?" he demanded. "We'll be seen as crazy. We could wreck the whole international economic order! Why don't we just forget the whole thing and let the chips fall where they may? Why should we put our necks out like this?"

Chan replied, "Don't buckle on me now! I need you to believe in what we're doing. What am I saying? This whole thing was your idea! You convinced me! Find your courage, my friend, because our conviction that this is the correct course is all that will get us through."

Chan hung up the phone and prepared for bed. He closed his eyes and was asleep in an instant. He dreamt he was sitting in his car still talking on the phone to James. In the near distance was a beautifully shaped mountain. The mountain seemed familiar, dressed as it was in snowy lace, but he couldn't quite place it. Somehow, right before his eyes, it transformed into a huge wave, crested on top with white foam. It was coming toward him. He informed James matter of factly, "I may lose you for a minute. There's an incredibly large tsunami headed toward my car."

The wave crashed all around him. Hurricane force winds blew away everything in their path. Large buildings swept past him on all sides. Chan was safe in his car as he witnessed the storm raging. He then found himself among his people. He calmly announced, "Don't be surprised if you see a change in the landscape when you look outside. A great wave and winds have washed away many buildings and trees. Only the strongest are left. But think how much better your view is now!"

The people looked out their windows and saw that Chan was right. The land was washed clean. The air was crisp and pure. The view was clear for miles.

When Chan awoke the next day, he knew what he would say to his people. He remembered the old adage Uncle Luang often repeated, "Cometh the hour, Cometh the man." He readied himself for his appearance before the nation. He began to write his speech.

"For the first time in China's 5,000 + year history, we have the power, the resources and the governmental authority to effect a major change in the world's economy. How we choose to use that power determines who we are as a people. As your leader I have enacted a 'day of Jubilee', a day of debt forgiveness, and have cancelled the one hundred trillion dollar debt owed to us by the United States of America. It may seem naive and foolish to perform an act of mercy and rescue another country by forgiving its huge debt. We are now facing a stagnant world economy. The reality is that without a thriving western market, China cannot sell its wares. If we cease to sell our wares, our economy will also fail. If you think of the world economy as a pyramid, you will find China at the top. That is only an enviable position if the base is strong and stable. Therefore, it must be acknowledged that in strengthening the position of other countries, we have the most to lose, but we also have the most to gain. In fact, our own survival ultimately depends on it.

Years ago, while living in America, I came to know a man who lived his life faithfully in accordance with the religion of Judaism. He taught me many lessons, including the ancient law of "Jubilee". It was a law that commanded the people to forgive all debts every fifty years. Now, when I am faced with the task of solving my country's serious economic troubles, I think back to that law and its practicality and wisdom.

What is the 'Jubilee' ethos? In observing 'Jubilee', the community comes together and acts selflessly for the good of all. We must expand the notion of community to include the community of nations, the world community. As we take the lead in an act of forgiveness, we set an example for others to follow. Is it always necessary for scores to be evened? It may not be possible to forget a major wrong which as been done or a huge debt which has been incurred. Yet, as long as we have the ability to forgive, we grant ourselves a new power, the power to move ahead without the burden of past resentments and a list of injustices needing to be redressed. Our largesse becomes a movement affecting all participants. This is a basic Buddhist principle. One's behavior is morally bound to affect oneself and those witnessing the behavior. Buddhists never see themselves operating outside a relationship. The relationship, not the individual or his acts, is paramount."

When he heard the speech broadcast across the country, Luang smiled to himself and nodded his head, knowing that all he had done to keep Chan safe and to help him thrive throughout his life had brought them to this glorious day. He felt a wave of calm and serenity throughout his being. He was at peace.

Sulee and Aro were amazed when they heard their president's announcement. They knew that this was Chan's good deed. They silently found each other's eyes and shared the pride that parents feel when they see their child go beyond their greatest expectations. They sought out their daughter and the Rozbruchs to celebrate.

At midnight, July 4th, 2033, on the fiftieth floor of a shining skyscraper overlooking the city of Beijing, a Chinese computer operator hit a button and the new balance statement of United States accounts payable to the People's Republic of China passed into American hands. It read $00.00. History had turned a page.

Chapter Forty-Four

The next morning, James walked through the White House corridors and into the Lincoln bedroom. He went to the window. As he watched the dawn, he sensed the sun rose with a superior luster. As president, there had been many occasions when his friendship with Chan had been severely criticized. People were increasingly suspicious. Why was an American president so close to the leader of the red Chinese? James wondered if his spectacular announcement would be seen as an attempt to refurbish his tarnished reputation. As this thought intruded on his immediate mission, he realized it was too late for doubts. The deed had been done. He must now guide the country to the future. He sat at the historic desk where many before him had gathered courage, and wrote his speech to the nation.

As the hour of reckoning drew close, James summoned his family. He wanted those he held dear standing near him during his address. He placed Sonia and Marie so close on his left side that he could feel their breath. Lilly and the children hovered on his right.

Minnie held Mark's hand as she was led to her place of honor directly behind her grandson, surrounded by Ruth, Sam, Dina and Eliana. James gathered all the love and good wishes around him and grew strong. His family watched in awe as the man they adored spoke to his countrymen.

My fellow Americans ...

Worldwide, the immediate reaction to the announcement was a

deep and contented sigh of appreciation. Finally, the two most powerful countries had demonstrated how mature leadership and benevolent cooperation could, in one bold stroke, ease troubled minds and souls. Though the future was still uncertain, it was heartening to witness the acknowledgment that nations needed to work together to tackle the enormous challenges before them.

Chapter Forty-Five

Many of the people who played a part in the recreation of the "Jubilee" were affected by dreams which moved them to act or to reevaluate their circumstances. There was one more dream to be had. This dream would be experienced by hundreds of millions of people. It's hard to imagine so many people having the same dream until it is realized that they were all awakened at the same time to the concept of a new spirit of mercy and generosity. James confirmed to his people that, if they sought it, benevolence could still be found, even in the most unlikely places. His trusted friend and ally led the way for his people to be "doubly blessed" by trusting their better instincts. Though the theme of liberty infused them all, each dream had a unique conception of what the future might be. Each was also imbued with a fervor which promised to fuel the needs of a new way of life.

James Gengia and Chan Khan knew that their people would have this dream. It was their plan all along to fulfill the hopes of their fellow countrymen and usher in a new day.

Made in the USA
Middletown, DE
27 May 2018